# The Last Ereph
# and Other Stories

JD Byrne

# DEDICATION

For Kelly, for making me think I can do this

# CONTENTS

1   Of That Alluring Fruit        1

2   To Watch the Storms          17

3   The Dragon of the Bailey     25

4   The Mask                     44

5   Jury Duty                    48

6   The Missing Legion           65

7   Fine Print                   79

8   Elephant Talk                94

9   Memory of Water              99

10  The Last Ereph              109

# Of That Alluring Fruit

My mother said that on the day I was born there was a brilliant blue sky overhead, streaked by only a few stray white clouds. It was unseasonably warm for late autumn, pleasant, and calm. Or so I was told, as I was too engaged in the process of being born to take notice.

Later I learned that the weather on the day of my birth was a good omen, a sign from the gods that my family had been blessed by my presence. In this land of deep, water-logged forests, where the sun shines only a few days each year, those who are sun births are said to be destined for great things.

My mother named me Kalsis, much to my father's dismay. It was an old family name, of no particular renown. My father would have named me after a great hunter or fearless protector, in order to curry further favor with the gods. Giving me the name Kalsis, he said, was a wasted opportunity that would cancel out the fortuity of my birth. But it did not matter. Mothers have the right to choose the names of their daughters, fathers of their sons. My father had no say in the matter.

~~~~~

My first memory is of the lake.

I was three or four years old. I had been in a fight with another child because he had done something to me. Thrown something at me or perhaps hit me. All I remember was being hurt, screaming, and crying. My mother came and scooped me up to calm me. She told me that sometimes I asked too many questions, and I had to learn how to keep them to myself. After she had taken me away from the incident, she put me down, took my hand in hers, and led me away from the village for a short walk.

When she let go of my hand, I ran, tearing through the forest south of our village. As my mother called after me, I came to the lake. It was a smooth, calm, almost unnaturally beautiful lake, the deepest blue I had ever seen and clear like a fine crystal. I ran down to the shore, my mother just behind, breathing hard. We stood for a few moments, in the quiet of a dull, grey day. She took my hand again and I began to relax, to put the incident behind me.

I looked out over the lake and saw the island that sat on the horizon, small and green, lingering at the edge of my vision. Far away, yet close enough to tantalize, to suggest that it lay within my reach. I could see one building on the island that was unlike any in our small village. It shone in the sun, brilliant white, with columns all around, and reminded me of something from a fairy story.

I did what any child would do. I found a rock, one just big enough to fit in the palm of my hand, and threw it hard, trying to hit the island. It flew out for only a few feet in a high, loping arc, before crashing into the surface, obliterating the stillness and creating ripples across the water.

My mother grabbed my shoulders, whipped me around to face her, and dropped to her knees to look directly into my eyes. "Do not ever do that again," she said in her sternest voice. "You must never do anything like that again. Don't come back here, ever, do you understand?" She stood, took my hand, and jerked me back in the direction of our village.

~~~~~

I became obsessed with the lake. When I had time to play after chores and lessons, I would sneak off through the woods, to the shore. Although I did not heed the spirit of my mother's words, I obeyed them to the letter. All I would do is walk down to the shore and watch the smooth crystal blue water remain impossibly calm. Sometimes I would sit on the grassy ground that bled into the water; other times I would simply stand for a few moments. I would look out at the island and its lone building, wondering what it was for, if anyone went there, and why. One day, when a hard rain blew in over the mountains, I ran to the lake to see what the pounding of the thousands of tiny drops would do to the surface. Aside from the initial impact, the lake seemed not to notice, absorbing the splashes without complaint.

One night, while a village festival was underway, I went to the shore, just to get away from the noise. The night was dark and cloudy, with little moonlight. Still, out on the island, there was a light. A slow, pulsing white light that looked as if it were alive had engulfed the building. It was like nothing I had ever seen before, like neither fire nor moonlight. I could only study it so long before I had to run back to the village, to the sound of my mother calling my name.

By the time I was 10 years old, I began to have more questions about the way our people avoided the lake with such care. I asked my brother, who was three years older, why was this lake so near our village always empty of people? Where were the fishermen? There was a much smaller pond in the forest where my friends and I would swim and fishermen would paddle their boats in search of a catch. But there were no boats on the lake. Did no one ever go to nor come from the island? And how did the water remain calm, even when the winds blew so hard that the trees in the forest rattled like some kind of furious percussion? He only shook his head and said, "Never go there, Kalsis. Anyone who tries to go to the island never returns."

My mother, who was responsible for my lessons while my father did his work in the forest, was no help in answering these questions. She repeated what my brother had told me, that no one who went to the island ever returned. But when I pressed her, asked her why, she could not say. At the time, I assumed the anger that flared in her was because she did not know the answers.

Ignorance can be frustrating, as I have learned. I know better now, but at the time, all I heard was my mother being furious at me for asking what, to me, were obvious questions.

One day, I asked my mother if I could go into the forest with my father. I told her I wanted to learn about what he did while we were at home. She was reluctant, but I talked to my father and convinced him it was a good idea. With trepidation, Mother let me go with Father to collect small game, the kind that he snared in traps strewn out in the forest.

It took a long time for my father and me to get to the area where his traps had been set. I did not mind the walk, picking through the damp undergrowth along a barely visible trail, because it gave me time to ask my father all the questions about the lake my mother could not, or would not, answer.

But he had no answers, only the same warning as my mother and brother. He admitted, with a sigh, that he did not know the answers. He did not know why there were no fishermen. He did not know why no boats came and went from the island. He did not know how the water remained so peaceful and undisturbed.

When I ran out of questions, just before we reached the area where the traps were set, my father stopped, took my hand, and looked down at me. "I know you have questions, Kalsis," he said, as if with a heavy heart, "and I have no answers. Just promise me, as you promised your mother, not to go to that lake."

I nodded, knowing it was the answer he needed. I knew, in my heart, it was a promise I had already broken many times, and one I could not keep.

~~~~~

In my village, the fourteenth anniversary of one's birth is a milestone. Not the passage into adulthood, but a significant step along the way. It is tradition that on a person's fourteenth birthday she can do anything she wants. I was prepared for this by not only my parents but my friends and my older brother. According to them, it was the best day of their lives and unlikely to be bettered. Once I realized what was to come, I knew what I wanted to do, what thing I wanted more than any other.

My mother woke me that morning and told me I could do anything I wished, but that I was to think hard about it. I would get only one choice and, once made, it could never be taken back. I would have all day to think about it, as I was to make my wish known that evening at the celebration feast.

That night, when the food was gone and the sun had given way to the dancing flames of a bonfire, my mother came to me and made a great spectacle of asking what I would like to do. "My dear daughter," she said, beaming in the firelight, "on this day, what is it that you wish more than anything?"

My heart broke before I even opened my mouth. "I want to go to the island in the lake," I said, as clearly and forcefully as I could.

The crowd, which until then had been a buzz of pleasant conversations, fell deathly silent.

My mother kept a smile on her face, forcing down her natural urge to shout at me, in order to downplay my insolence before the others. "Dear Kalsis, you know that is impossible," she said, chuckling slightly. "Because that request must have been made in good humor, I will pretend I did not hear it." The assembled crowd took a moment, then applauded my mother's grace. "So, now, tell me truly, Daughter, what is it that you wish more than anything?"

I swallowed hard, stood my ground, and tried not to let the stares of dozens of eyes shake my resolve. "I want to go to the island," I said. "If, on this day of all days, I am permitted to do as I please, than surely you cannot deny me this?" My words hung in the air, with only the crackling of the bonfire to accompany them. In the silence and the stares, I weakened just a bit. "But if this wish cannot be granted, I wish for you to tell me why it cannot be so."

For the longest time, my mother said nothing. I could not tell if she was actually shocked that I would make such a request or was furiously thinking of what to do about it. Finally, she said, "Daughter, I cannot choose your wish for you. You have said what you want, and I must tell you it cannot be."

"Then what of my other wish?" I asked. "Tell me the reason why I cannot have this."

"No," she said, shaking her head and walking away. "There is only one wish. You made your request. I am sorry that it is something that cannot be granted."

I could tell that my mother was seething for what I had done, for doing it in such a public way. But that was the opportunity I thought best to get answers to all those questions. If I was to have them, I would have to get them another way.

~~~~~

After my fourteenth birthday had come and gone, I threw myself, with grim determination, into the task of becoming a strong swimmer. Every morning and every afternoon, after I had rushed through my lessons, I went to the pond and swam the length and breadth of it over and over.

My friends played in the shallow waters, or took up fishing, as they grew older. They did not see the point of my daily regimen. It was not fun, they noted, just to swim back and forth. Now and then one of them, usually one of the boys, would challenge me to a race. But contests posed no challenge, because I had built up my body and my technique to slice through the water like a fish, while my opponent would slap and splash at it like a drowning man. After a while, they left me to my solitary pursuit, although I am sure they said unkind things about me when I was not listening.

So I swam, alone, every day that I could. In the heat of midsummer, in the rain, and sometimes even in the cold of winter, unless it was snowing. Only when the ice made swimming impossible did I forgo my training.

~~~~~

In my life, the twentieth year was one of transition. I was no longer a child, having attained nineteen years and adulthood. However, I was also not yet truly independent and not expected to worry about marrying and starting my own family until my next birthday. The twentieth year is one of freedom and exploration, the time during which young men and women are to find their true calling.

For me, my twentieth year was the time I knew I had to make a bold decision. If I did not act on the plan I had carried in my head for all those years, I would never be able to. My dream would be covered over by the debris of adult life, of marriage and motherhood. In my twentieth year, I was beholden to no one else. My mother and father cared for me, of course, but they knew the way of the world and knew it was time to release me. I had no husband, nor even a suitor, much less children. Free of entanglements, this was my time.

One summer day, I awoke to a clear blue sky and knew that day would be my chance. I slipped away from the village unnoticed when the cloudy skies broke and golden rays of sun warmed the forest. A rare sunny day, like the day of my birth, would send the village into a festive and playful mood. Chores would be skipped, lessons postponed. The routine of life would change, for at least a little while. In the din, nobody would notice one person missing, especially one to whom little thought was given in the first instance.

I made my way to the shore of the lake quickly and cautiously, stopping every few moments to make sure no one was following. The water was, as always, perfectly still and serene. No waves lapped upon the shore. The glassy surface was never broken by a fish surfacing or an insect dancing across the water. The island sat there as it always had, just on the edge of the horizon, its single building blazing white in the afternoon sun. I slipped off my sandals and dipped one foot into the water, expecting it to be as chilled as the pond back in the forest. But the water was warm, inviting, and completely comfortable. I stepped in with my other foot and stood, for a moment, drinking in the surroundings.

I turned back, one last time, to look at the dense trees behind me. Maybe I was hoping for someone to appear, to run to me, to stop me from doing what I was about to do. But no one came and, resolved, I turned back to the lake. I stepped out of the water, stripped off my clothes, and laid them neatly on a rock near the tree line. I walked into the water, moving slowly out into the lake until the water rose past my waist. With one last foot on solid ground beneath me, I pushed off and dove headlong out into the lake, toward the island.

I tried to settle into an easy rhythm, slipping one arm into the water in front of me, then the other, keeping tempo with the slow kicks of my feet. But the water felt odd, nothing like what I had swum through all those days in the pond. It remained calm, broken only by my rotating arms and kicking legs, and began to congeal around me. It was as if the water itself was developing hands that grasped at me as I struggled to slip through it.

I battled against this newly deployed force. It was not a barrier, something ahead of me to break through. Rather, it was pulling at me, as if trying to drag me back to the shore of the lake. Back to my village. Back to the rest of my life. I fought against it, whatever this was that would hold me back. My arms moved more slowly, more deliberately, than before, developing more force. I took a deep breath every time my mouth broke the surface. My legs kicked dutifully, refusing to be held in place.

What I had thought would be easy quickly turned to a struggle. This was not exhaustion. I knew what it felt like to be out of energy, short of breath with muscles burning under my skin. That was not what I was feeling.

Soon, the island grew in my vision every time I opened my eyes. I was so close I could almost feel the soft green grass under my feet. But as I drew closer, the character of the water around me began to change. It began to thin out and feel more like what water should be. The force that had been pulling me backward slowly faded. Quickly, I settled into an easy rhythm. Based on my experience in the pond, I thought I would be able to reach the island, if not make it there and back, without worry.

I cruised through the water, almost effortlessly, for several minutes. I varied the rhythm of my breathing just enough so that I could lift my whole head from the water and keep an eye on the island, making sure I was heading in the right direction. It grew slowly in front of me, the familiar blotch of green and white remaining frustratingly out of focus. There was no point in stopping and treading water for a moment to get a good look. No point in wasting energy I might need later.

In a few moments I began to see the land of the island with some detail. Rocks. Dirt. Small flowers poking up through the grass. I was so close, but the swim had been harder than I expected. I was not about to be stopped now. As I reached the shore, my right hand shot out and slammed, hard, onto solid earth. This was not the slowly sloping bottom of the lake; this was the soil of the island itself. I dug my fingers into the dirt, then did the same with my other hand.

With one last great effort, I hoisted myself out of the water, which clung to me like a desperate lover. I threw myself onto the ground, gasping for air, trying to recover my strength and my wits. I turned to look for some evidence of the force that had held me back, but there was nothing to see. Just the calm, still blue water of the lake. I closed my eyes and let a great feeling of weariness wash over me.

~~~~~

The sun had set by the time I awoke, yet it was not quite dark. The blazing orange had been replaced by what I thought was the pale glow of a full moon. The heat of the summer day had been replaced by the brisk chill of an autumn night, like the heat had all been sucked away. The breeze blowing in across the lake cut through my naked body like a frozen knife. I stood up and wrapped my arms around my shoulders, preserving what warmth I had in me.

Though it was pale, the light was bright enough to allow me to see my surroundings and walk up the hill from the lake. The grass under my feet was soft and not yet slick with dew. The ground was remarkably even and smooth. I kept expecting a rock or a sharp bit of a plant or even some animal to squirm out from under foot, but none ever materialized. I continued toward the building I had seen from afar all these years.

To my surprise, there was no more to the island than I had seen from the shore. The spot I had looked upon all those years was not some random outcropping, jutting out from a larger piece of land. It was all there was, with only a few dozen yards of gently sloping green grass between the lake and the building in the center of the island.

Nor did the single structure match the picture I had crafted of it in my mind, based on all those looks from so far away. It was a circle, between one and two hundred paces around. It was not connected to any other structure. No road led to it or away from it. The land simply sloped away from the building gently, down to the lake, on all sides, with nothing to distinguish one side from the other.

What I had thought from the shore were columns, holding up the building's elegantly arched roof, were not columns at all, at least not the kind I had learned about in my lessons. Instead of being made from polished white marble, they were light grey in color and shone like polished metal. They stood in close ranks with one another and were connected at the top by slight strands of something I did not recognize. If the building had been a ruin, ravaged by the ages as it sat unkempt, I would have called them vines or weeds that had made this place their home. But there was no ruin here. Everything was neat and clean. Even the grass was short and orderly, free of weeds.

As I had been wrong about the columns, so too was I wrong about the light by which I was able to make these observations. It was not the pale light of the full moon overhead. In fact, when I looked up, there was no moon at all, the sky a mix of black and grey clouds, with only a few visible stars. The light was coming from inside the building. As I walked around outside, I could feel the heat of the light seep slowly into my skin, into my body, deep down into my bones. The chill of the breeze dissolved in the soft white light. I slowly let my arms fall to my side instead of clutching myself trying to keep out the cold.

I walked all the way around the building twice before I noticed an opening, something like a doorway, between two of the columns. I swore to myself that it had not been there before, but there was no way to be sure. Everything on the island looked so similar that I had lost my bearings and could not have found my way back home. I turned and looked behind me, but could not make out the shore of the mainland in the dark. So far as I knew, there was nothing in the world except the lake and the island. The light from inside the building seemed to grow, slowly, and was pulsing, as if struggling to get out.

I turned back to the opening, which was now a blaze of light outlined by thin black lines of metal. All my life I had wondered what was on this island, who was on this island. I wondered who had built this magnificent structure and why it was here. The answers to all my questions seemed to scream at me from inside. I did the only thing I could do.

I walked into the light.

~~~~~

Now I have my answers. I know that the island is not actually an island. It is a great, expansive beast from some other place, another world. I know that it came here eons ago, when the barely sentient beings in the forest nearby had just begun to walk upright. I know that its arrival here left a great crater, into which rain fell to produce the lake. I know that the beast keeps the waters so calm so as to catch the eye of passersby. I know the great beast can do nothing to return from whence it came. It cannot move. I know that it sits and watches in silence.

I know this because I am part of the beast now. A small part, as are dozens of others who were once like me, young and curious about the world around them.

Children who asked questions and received no good answers. Who were pulled to the lake shore, into the still waters. Who were driven to the island and what was contained in the gleaming building that sat atop it.

And so we came. The beast took us into itself. We sustain it and it sustains us, over all this time, feeding off our need to know more. We learn about the beast's world while it learns about ours. Those that I knew in my old life – my mother and father, my brother, the ones I called friends – are long gone. Even their descendents have, in most instances, left this place.

There are so few left now. They keep to themselves. No one comes to the lake. No one gazes out at the island sitting atop the calm waters. No one wonders any more. The curiosity that I and those who came before me share is gone. What has sustained us all for so long is slipping away. The beast remains silent, as it always has. Those of us who have sustained the beast for all this time do not talk about it, either, for fear of knowing what it might mean for our own fates.

But I am curious.

# To Watch the Storms

The timing was perfect. The heavy, grey clouds had been building for the last 30 miles, but the rain held off until we pulled into the hotel. It was going to get ugly and it was good to be off the road.

Alek stopped the car, slammed the transmission into park, and waited for the valet to come running. "I'm sorry," he said, continuing a conversation we'd been having for an hour, "you just can't convince me."

"But what about all those eyewitnesses," I said. "People who don't have any reason to lie all tell stories, very similar stories, about seeing UFOs." I hopped out of the car and grabbed my briefcase from the back.

"Hmpf," Alek said as he handed the valet the keys. "Given our line of work, you should be more skeptical of eyewitnesses. You know how unreliable they are. Remember the Martin case we had a few years back?"

I did. I remembered how the victim was completely sure our client had attacked her, but then DNA testing showed he was in another state at the time. Still, I wasn't ready to let this go. "Juries still tend to think they're reliable," I said, "no matter how many times we tell them."

"Exactly," Alek said, grabbing his suitcase and wheeling it into the lobby. "Besides, aren't the people who see those things a little, you know." He made the universal sign for crazy by circling a finger near his forehead.

"Whatever," I said, letting the matter drop so that we could get down to the business of checking in. Once we were done, Alek got off the elevator two floors before me. "Dinner in a couple hours?" I asked. He nodded and wandered off down the hallway.

I found my room and began the usual routine for a court visit. I turned on the TV and opened the drapes wide. The window looked out over the older section of downtown in this smallish southern city. It was bigger than home, but only by a little bit. New York City or Chicago, it was not. The hotel, and the attached office tower, were the tallest buildings in this part of the city, rising over the refurbished warehouses that dated back to just after the Civil War.

When I travel for work, I like to get a sense of what's happening around the city, so I tuned to one of the local newscasts and started unpacking. There was nothing all that interesting going on, just the usual petty crime and politics. I hung my suit in the closet and was stuffing some underwear in a dresser drawer, but my attention was drawn to what was going on outside.

The storm rolled up on the city even more quickly than I expected. The last breaths of day had been strangled under dark clouds. In the distance, over the worn and battered roof tops towards the river, I could see the occasional flash of lightning. The clouds seemed impossibly low, almost near the level of my window, but I chalked that up to a trick of the light and returned to unpacking.

The weather guy was clearly giddy about the line of thunderstorms they were tracking, gesturing gravely at a pixelated, brightly colored blob on the radar. He repeated several times that there had been a tornado reported, which made him entirely too excited. I chuckled and laid out my razor, comb, and toothbrush in the bathroom.

When I came out, whatever bit of daylight that had lingered was gone. The lightning was more intense and moving directly towards the hotel. Quickly. This was shaping up to be quite a storm, maybe even as bad as the weather guy was predicting. Low, grey clouds were sliding into place, punctuated by the dull glow of heat lightning. The trees on the street down below were in constant motion, swaying back and forth. I turned off the TV (didn't care about local sports, anyway) and walked to the window.

I heard the initial rumble of thunder. It was close, but not right on top of the hotel. Not yet. The wind was also picking up, buffeting the window with just enough force to be noticed.

Then came the first real strike of lightning, zipping down from the clouds towards a refurbished row house about four blocks away. Another clap of thunder followed, louder this time. It was just on the verge of being frightening. The rain pouring out of the rolling clouds looked like a fine mist at this distance. Another burst of lightning, this one setting off several subsidiary flashes in the clouds themselves. They were still very low. I wondered how low thunderclouds could get. I had never seen them like this.

The wind was really howling now. This side of the hotel wasn't flat, but rather composed of rooms and windows that jutted out from the walls at odd angles. The wind whipped around those exposed places, collected in the recessed bits, then exploded back out into the atmosphere. The result was an unnerving low-level hum, like the synthesized drone in the background of an avant-garde art installation.

The storm was almost on top of the hotel now, hunching over the next block like a massive fuzzy spider. Another flash of lightning. The accompanying thunder clap sounded like an explosion. It must have rattled the windows, but I couldn't hear them over the wind.

In another moment, the clouds, storm, and rain had arrived at the hotel. Water lashed against the window, blown sideways by the wind. A flash of lightning appeared to shoot down right into the parking building directly across the street. This time, the thunder boomed like it was out in the hallway, and the windows definitely rattled.

I just stood there, dumbfounded, taking in the sights and sounds. The increasingly vibrant light show. The violent winds. The buckets of water slamming against the building next door so hard it looked like they were shot out of some immense cannon.

As the clouds enveloped the hotel, my eyes were drawn to something deep in the heart of them. It looked like lightning, or the reflections of lightning, giving a glow to the dark mist. Only it wasn't flashing.

It was moving. And not in a windblown way, not like something caught up in the swirling breezes and tossed about without reason. It moved with purpose. It zipped quickly one way, then the other, in spite of the blustering wind. Then it climbed and dove in smooth arcs.

And there were two of them.

I squinted, trying to get a better focus on the objects that were darting in and out of the clouds. They would emerge out of the top of the cloud like a dolphin jumping in the ocean, then plunge back inside. One after the other, almost like they were chasing each other. Like they were . . . playing.

Lightning flashed right in front of me. Right below me, actually, since the cloud was wrapped around the hotel like a mink stole. The flash was so bright I instinctively turned away, trying to shield my eyes. But it was too late. I shook my head and the blinding white afterimage slowly disappeared. Thunder shook the building. The lights flickered, but the power was still on.

When my eyesight returned, I looked back out the window. Hanging in midair right in front of my window were a pair of small, perfectly smooth, teardrop-shaped objects. They looked like glistening steel. In fact, they looked like spaceships from a science fiction movie, but they were only the size of a prop. Each was maybe a foot long.

The two objects hovered there, improbably, not being swayed by the wind or rain at all. One of them turned to its left, sideways to the window, as if to let me see the tiny craft in profile. The other zipped off without warning, charging up and away from the window.

"Holy shit," I said, before something clicked in my brain. "Alek has to see this." I dashed over to the bed, grabbed my cell phone, and punched his number. It rolled over to voice mail. Twice. He was probably asleep, passed out on his bed like at the end of every one of these long drives. I switched to text. "Come up here now! Rm 7013! At least look outside!" I didn't expect a response, but it was worth a shot.

At the window, the ship that stayed behind moved slowly closer, sidling up to the window. As it got closer, I could see a portal on the side, a small, round, reinforced window, no more than a couple inches or so in diameter. It was the only blemish on the otherwise perfectly smooth surface. I squinted again, trying to look inside. It moved closer, until I could see a tiny creature inside. He looked just like one of those creatures from *Close Encounters* or *Communion*. A long skinny body, topped by an oversized head, all covered in grey. There was no mouth, but giant black eyes.

He blinked.

I blinked back.

Below the ship I could see that the storm was clearing. I looked back at the ship just long enough to catch the eyes of the little pilot. With both hands, he was grasping a device that looked like the steering wheel of a Formula One race car, covered with tiny knobs, switches, and lights. He took one hand off the wheel, and waved, slowly, at me.

I waved back, then fumbled with my phone, trying to get the camera on. My fingers slipped and brought up the calendar instead. I cursed and looked back out the widow.

The little pilot put his hand back on the wheel. By the time I got the camera working, the ship had taken off, following the trajectory of its counterpart. The chase, it appeared, was on again. I took a few seconds of video as the ship race away, but knew I hadn't caught anything aside from the rain and grey sky.

The storm cleared out as quickly as it had come. It was early enough in the evening that the sun came back out for just a few minutes. On the way down in the elevator, I played back the brief video I'd been able to take, but there was nothing to see other than dreary grey mist.

Alek was waiting in the lobby when I went down for dinner, swiping repeatedly at the screen of his phone. After a perfunctory discussion about dinner, he said, "So what was so important? Called *and* texted. Must have been something."

In my pocket, my hand wrapped around my phone like it was a talisman, proof of the most wondrous thing ever that even Alek couldn't dismiss. I toyed with the idea of showing it to him, to convince him of what I had seen with my own damned eyes.

"Turned out it was nothing," I said, finally, letting it go. "Just a neat storm, you know?"

"Pfft," he said, with theatrical flourish, "you've seen one storm you've seen 'em all. Nothing but water, darkness, and junk blowing around."

"Yeah," I said, "I guess I just get drawn into them sometimes."

We crossed the street and the conversation shifted again. As we walked, I kept looking up into the evening sky, wondering when the next storm would come.

# The Dragon of the Bailey

Lhai sniffed the water in his trough. Was the poison in there? He couldn't tell. He cursed, not for the first time, that the Maker had given dragons such a poor sense of smell. What if he just didn't drink it? How could they make him? He was as large as any of the guards. Bigger, if one counted his tail. His rough grey hide would be difficult for spears or swords to pierce. What could they do if he would not drink? But how could he refuse when he was so very thirsty?

He extended his wings, stretching nearly six feet from end to end. The cobalt blue feathers had come in fuller and thicker this time. It had been easy for him to swoop up to the perch yesterday afternoon, probably too easy. If he had resisted the urge to be away from these humans for a while, to sit above them and keep watch on their activities, maybe his keeper would have forgotten about the clipping. Another few days and perhaps he could have flown over the wall and away from this bailey. But his regular water and food disappeared a few days ago and the keeper would not let Lhai out of his sight. The clipping was near. His keeper was not so forgetful.

But now it was too late, and he was so very thirsty. He drove his head into the trough and gulped furiously, knowing that a deep sleep would soon overtake him.

~~~~~

When he woke up, Lhai could feel the cold iron and leather muzzle that had been wrapped around his face for the ceremony. It took a few moments before he realized where he was and for the throbbing pain in his wings to come to the fore. He gritted his teeth and tried to stand, but was stopped by a sharp yank on the chain that lashed him to the stone pedestal.

To one side, keeping a safe distance, was a priest. He held a large, worn, brown book in his hands and smiled nervously at Lhai when their eyes met.

To the other side, at the same distance but looking much more certain of himself, sat the one they called Lord Kala. He looked bored by the state of affairs, as if he had something better to do. Lhai hoped his unconsciousness had delayed the proceedings, just to be difficult.

Out in front of him, Lhai could see the crowd that had gathered in the courtyard below, huddled together against the chill of the damp morning mist that was so prevalent in these parts. There were a few dozen people, ringed by another dozen guards in polished armor, creating a makeshift fence out of tall, golden spears. What the Maker had taken from the nose, She had given to the ear, but the crowd murmured to itself, making it difficult for Lhai to hear the contents of any one conversation.

The crowd hushed when the priest raised the book high over his head and began to intone the prayer. Lhai had heard it six times before, every year on the anniversary of his capture, a day that also happened to be Kala's birthday. For Kala, the coincidence made Lhai's captivity all the more auspicious.

"And so the Maker, who is just and gracious," the priest said, slowly and deliberately, "did promise that should any dragon come to your castle, then should you know peace and happiness."

"Get on with it," Kala said, slumped in his chair.

The priest picked up the pace, as ordered. "And so long as the dragon remains in your castle, the lord of that castle shall rule, with justice and mercy to his people." The lines were well worn and got little reaction from the scrum.

As the priest continued, Lhai's eyes caught some movement near the back of the crowd. He focused on a young boy, no more than nine years old, tugging urgently on the arm of the old man who stood beside him.

"Grandfather," the boy said, in a loud whisper that was drowned out by the priest's speech for everyone save Lhai. The old man tried to shush him, but the boy kept on. "Why does it wear a muzzle? Why is it chained down? If it wants to stay, why does it . . .," the boy asked, before the old man put an end to it with a swift smack up the side of his head.

Lhai grinned, as best he could.

~~~~~

27

One benefit to having his wings clipped was that, for a few weeks afterward, Lhai was free to roam the bailey without much oversight. Each day he would struggle up to his perch on the inner wall and survey the activities of the humans.

He kept an eye out in particular for the boy who had so many questions. Lhai watched one day as the boy ran with great purpose to and fro around the bailey, slipping in between people twice his size. He was not playing; he was working, apparently as a runner for someone. He knew this place well, better than a boy of his age should.

One day, when the boy stopped by the well for a drink, Lhai flapped awkwardly down from his perch and landed on the stone wall of the well, a few feet away. The boy did his best to avoid looking his direction.

"You work hard, boy," Lhai said, trying his best to smooth out the natural rasp in his voice.

The boy turned to him, his eyes wide and mouth agape. He quickly looked away and took another drink.

"Now, now," Lhai said, shuffling along the wall toward the boy, "there is no need to worry. I am not going to hurt you."

The boy stopped drinking, like he was mulling over the proposition, but did not look at the dragon.

"I know you have questions. How can I answer them if you will not talk to me, boy?"

"Lessard," the boy said, after a deliberative pause. "My name is Lessard."

"Ah, he speaks! You may call me Lhai, Lessard. So, what do you want to know?"

Lessard looked around to see if anyone was watching them. "Grandfather says you are dangerous, to stay away."

Lhai sat back on his haunches, doing his best to look like an oversized mongrel dog rather than a dragon. "Do I look dangerous to you?"

They continued like this, talking a bit every day when the boy stopped to get a drink. One day, Lessard leaned in particularly close. "Can you breathe fire?"

Lhai grinned. "What do you think?"

"My grandfather told me so," Lessard said. "A single dragon could burn an entire village down."

"If I could breathe fire, why would I still be here?" Lhai asked. "Your grandfather has, no doubt, heard many things in his long life and is most wise, but not everything he has heard is the truth."

Lessard looked indignant. "Are you calling him a liar?"

"No, no, young friend," Lhai said, in his best soothing voice. "One need not be a liar to be wrong about something, only misinformed. That is no sin." He thought otherwise, actually, but he could not antagonize the boy.

Over the days, Lessard asked more questions borne of his grandfather's tales.

"Do you live forever?" he asked one dreary afternoon.

"No, of course not," Lhai said. "Everything must come to an end. That is the way the Maker made the world. But we do live a very long time, compared to humans."

"How do you remember it all?" Lessard asked. "Your whole long life?"

"The Maker has blessed us with great memories," Lhai said. "Once we have seen something, or heard someone say something, we will never forget it. One day, long in the future, when you are as old as your grandfather, I will remember our talks perfectly."

Another day, Lessard asked if Lhai had a store of treasure buried somewhere deep in a mountain.

Lhai chuckled. "Not all dragons live in mines or caves," he said. "We do like to live apart from each other and apart from humans. But, yes, your grandfather is right about the treasure. Live a long life and you, too, will accumulate many things." He did not mention that his own cache was surely gone now, with no one to protect it all these years.

One time, it was Lhai who asked the questions. "You always talk of your grandfather," he asked, "but what of your mother or father?"

Lessard took a slow drink. "My father was killed. In one of Lord Kala's battles. It was a long time ago, just after I was born."

Lhai did his best to look sympathetic. "And your mother?"

Lessard stared into the well for a long time. "She's gone."

"Gone?"

"Just gone," Lessard said, walking away.

Finally, one day when the clinging rain of the morning finally came to an end, Lessard asked the question Lhai had been hoping and waiting for. "If you have wings, why don't you fly away?"

Lhai hopped down off of the well and spread his wings wide, partly blocking the sunlight. "Look closely at these wings, Lessard. What do you see?"

The boy scanned the bailey, cautiously, to see if anyone else was looking, then stepped closer and peered at Lhai's left wing. "Feathers," he said. "Like a bird. So you should be able to fly."

Lhai nodded. "Look closer. Does something look wrong about them?" He waved the left wing around a bit.

Lessard backed away. "They're so short. Why?"

"Because," he said, wrapping his wings down along his back, "they are clipped every few weeks, to keep them that way."

"Who does that?" Lessard asked, a puzzled look on his face.

"My keeper," Lhai said. "I do not know his name. But I do know he does it on the orders of Lord Kala."

Lessard stood there, mouth partly open but saying nothing, for a few seconds. "Why would Lord Kala do that?"

Lhai moved a bit closer and whispered, "Because if my feathers grew back completely, I would be able to fly away from here."

"But," Lessard started to say, then stopped himself. "But, you stay here because it is the Maker's blessing upon Lord Kala's reign."

Lhai slowly shook his head. "If it is truly the Maker's will that I remain here, why must Lord Kala do this?" He unfurled his wings again. "I am a prisoner, Lessard, just as much as the petty thieves in the dungeon. It makes no difference that I am not chained every day. What is Lord Kala afraid of?"

Lessard said nothing more, only took another long drink, then ran off. Lhai flapped awkwardly back up to his perch on the wall and smiled, just slightly. He didn't want anyone else to think he might be pleased.

~~~~~

That night the full moon was obscured by passing clouds, casting a shifting white glow over the castle. Lhai had settled into an empty cart, enjoying its soft straw, when he saw a figure walking across the bailey. It was Lessard, doing his best to move without arousing suspicion.

"Psst, boy!" Lhai said in a loud whisper. "Lessard!"

The boy changed course and jogged silently to the wagon.

"What are you doing up at this time of night?" Lhai asked.

In the pale moonlight, Lessard's young face looked tense and haggard. "I can't sleep. Can't keep from thinking about," he said, nodding toward Lhai's folded wings.

"Thank you," the dragon said, "but it is not your concern, you know."

"It is," Lessard said, passionately. "The priests and grandfather say that what Lord Kala does, he does on all our behalf."

Lhai decided to play along. "Still, you are just a young boy. I appreciate your sympathy, but . . ."

Lessard shook his head to cut him off. "This is wrong," he declared firmly. "They shouldn't do that to anybody, what they do to you."

Lhai tried hard not to grin widely at the boy. He had come around more quickly that he could have hoped. "But what can you do against the strength of Lord Kala and his men?"

The boy thought for a moment. "How long would it take for your feathers to grow back? All the way back, I mean?"

"Not long, perhaps another week," Lhai said, "but they will get clipped again in a few days."

"And once your feathers have grown back, you can fly away?"

Lhai nodded. "Yes, I think so. It has been so long since I have truly flown, but I think I could."

"Then all we need is a place to hide you," Lessard said. "Let me think about it." He turned and left without another word.

Two nights later, Lessard again came to Lhai while he rested in the cart. "I've found a place," he said, waving the dragon to follow him.

Lhai dutifully obliged, trailing Lessard to a spot where one of the bailey's inner walls met the high rock wall that defined the castle. The boy fell to his knees and clawed earth out from the foot of the wall with his hands. In a few moments he had a small hole dug, big enough to wiggle lose a stone in the inner wall.

"There," he said, pointing to the hole in the wall.

Lhai crouched down and peered inside, slipping his long neck into the hole. "What is that?"

"It's a back room, locked behind a heavy wooden door, in the blacksmith's shop. It's storage. I don't think he's been there in years." Lessard looked at the dragon. "It's a place for you to hide."

Lhai examined the hole again. It was small, but he could fit through it, with some effort. "All right," he said. "Then what?"

"You stay there as long as it takes for your feathers to grow back," Lessard said. "Then I'll let you out and you can fly away."

It seemed very simple when the boy said it. "Will they not come and look there?" Lhai gestured toward the hole and the small room beyond it.

Lessard grinned. "Trust me. I've spent a lot of time in that room. If you don't want to be found, that's the place."

Lhai looked around and considered his options. "I suppose there is no reason to wait then, eh?" He began to shimmy his way through the hole. It was a tighter fit that he imagined, the rough edges of the stone scraping against his hide as he went through. It wasn't pleasant, but he could do it again, when the time came.

"How long should I wait?" Lessard asked, already piling the dirt back into position, as if closing the last spot of Lhai's tomb.

"A week," Lhai said, "but no more. I will be starving by then."

"A week," Lessard agreed, then slowly moved the stone back into the hole.

~~~~~

The room was cold, dark, and damp, but it suited Lhai's purpose. It was such an unpleasant place, he couldn't imagine anyone making more than a cursory examination of it. He felt bad for Lessard, who must be very eager for solitude to subject himself to it.

The walls were made of stacked stones, between which there were numerous cracks and crevices. It was not enough to light the room, but enough sunlight filtered through for Lhai to mark the passing of the days. It also allowed enough sound to seep through that Lhai could follow the goings on outside.

The hue and cry had gone up in the morning after Lessard hid him, not long after the sun rose. There was shouting and the sound of pounding feet running all around the bailey. The next day there must have been an assembly of some kind, as Lhai heard Lord Kala address his subjects. He called for calm in this moment of uncertainty. When someone asked what it meant that the dragon was missing, Kala said only that "it means dragons are very willful creatures. That is why its choosing to live here brings with it the Maker's blessing."

Fearing that his sanctuary might be discovered, Lhai went to a long, low bench that ran along the far wall. He was able to reposition the items stored underneath it and slide into the empty space. With his teeth he pulled a ragged blanket up over him. He made himself as small, as still, and as quiet as possible. Then he waited.

In his hiding place, deep within an already well hidden room, Lhai began to lose track of time. He didn't know whether it was later that same day or the next when the guards came. First he heard a mass of voices. There was so much commotion in the bailey, he didn't pick them out specifically at first, but he heard them growing closer and clearer.

Finally, he heard a baritone voice, the captain of Kala's guard, berating someone on the other side of the door, charging him with the most grave of offenses. Lhai took a deep breath and tried as best he could to squeeze into an even smaller space.

The door thundered open, thudding hard against one of the many bits of furniture and debris piled around the room.

"In there!" shouted the captain, "what's in there?"

"Just junk," said the blacksmith, voice fluttering nervously. Lhai almost felt bad for him.

Feet moved in and around the room, heavy steps clomping on the dirt floor. There were several guards, at least three, plus the one who had been yelling. Lhai heard one of the guards step not six inches away from him. Instinctively, he flinched, enough that the blanket fell away, partly exposing his head.

One pair of feet turned and walked toward the bench, beside which another pair stood, motionless. Lhai swallowed hard, his heart pounding in his ears, then heard a loud thump from above him.

"What's that?" he heard the captain say. The blacksmith said nothing. "Don't you know that Lord Kala has prohibited any idols of the old gods? You're not a blasphemer, are you?"

"No, no, of course not," said the blacksmith. "It's just a token. A family heirloom, really. My father's father, you see . . ." He was cut off by what sounded like a smack across the face.

"Yes, well, we'll have to take it with us," the guard said. "Anything else?"

The two standing in front of Lhai murmured to each other, and then to the captain, that there was nothing else here.

"Right, then, let's get out of here," the captain said.

Lhai watched as the feet only a few inches from him turned and marched back toward the door. In short order it slammed closed again and Lhai felt the fear and tension melt away from him. He didn't know how much more of this he could take.

~~~~~

Lhai stayed stock still in his hiding place, curled up so tightly that he shook. His throat was dry and his stomach ached. Every noise made him clench and catch his breath. He lost track of the days. How much longer before Lessard would come to let him out? When he heard the guards return and rough up the blacksmith just outside the door, he knew he could wait no longer.

Once they were gone, Lhai emerged from his refuge and carefully felt his way around the wall, searching for the loose block. When he found the one that just ever so slightly jutted out from the wall, he took a tenuous hold of it with his talons and began to pull. The rock was dry and slick and his talons slipped off, sending him tumbling backwards. He redoubled his efforts, working more carefully to pry the block slowly out of its spot.

When the block was moved, he began to dig, throwing great heaps of dirt behind him. He could hear the sound of voices around, but did not give them much attention. Light began to creep through the hole the more earth he moved. It was daytime, not the best time for an escape. Never mind – he could take no more of this.

When the hole was big enough, Lhai dove in, head first. It was a tight fit, but he managed to make it through, bursting out of the other side to see a gathering of people staring at him.

"The dragon!" murmured the crowd, wide smiles beginning to blossom on the faces.

Lhai knew he had only a few moments before Kala's men would come to put him in chains. It was time to do two things he had not done in all the years he had been held captive.

First, he took in a deep breath and unleashed a high, ragged, piercing shriek. It drove some of the assembled throng running, while others covered their ears. The smiles instantly disappeared. The mass of humanity stepped back, giving Lhai more room. It would surely bring the out the guards, but they would be coming anyway. Either he escaped now or not at all.

Second, he raised his wings and extended them fully, sweeping the air in front of him and driving the crowd back a bit more. He took a quick glimpse left and right and smiled. With great up and down strokes Lhai beat his wings and slowly began to lift off the ground, quickly gaining momentum. He shrieked again, just for good measure.

Lhai rose into the air, more easily than he had in years. His wings ached, sending shots of pain down his back. He gritted his teeth and beat them again, trying to push through the hot aching of muscles that had lain dormant for so long. Drawn by the commotion, a squad of Kala's guards ran across the bailey and stared, mouths open, as Lhai rose slowly, five feet then ten feet into the air.

Lhai caught a glimpse of something shiny, the sun glinting off metal, out of the corner of his eye. He turned and saw one of the guards notching an arrow in his bow. Lhai beat his wings harder and began to make for the wall. He needed another fifteen feet to clear it, but he could feel his weight dragging behind him.

"You idiot!" the captain shouted.

Lhai looked over his shoulder and saw the captain smacking the bow out of the guard's hand. "We've just found it and now you want to kill it?"

Lhai smirked, knowing that a single arrow could not kill him, but if it somehow happened to pierce his hide it would slow him down, which he couldn't afford right now. He took a deep breath and drove, with all his strength, toward the top of the outer wall. He rose higher and higher – first to the level of his perch, then to the top of the rampart - as he closed in on the wall. But he realized, nearly too late, that he did not yet have the height to carry him over.

Before he hit the wall, Lhai executed a long banked turn, so that he faced the bailey and the assembled crowd below. He stopped beating his wings and began to fall, just for a split second. Then he extended them again and swooped down over the bailey, plunging toward the crowd. The dive both caused them to scatter and gave Lhai needed speed. It also allowed him to see Lessard, hiding from the rushing crowd near the well. Lhai tried to give him a nod, some kind of acknowledgement, but he also saw some of the guard hustling back to the bailey with ropes and nets.

Lhai knew this was his last chance. He dove down to about five feet, gaining speed as he went, then banked hard back up toward the outer wall. He beat his wings with swift, powerful strokes, gaining height as he charged to the wall. The smooth, dry fibers of a rope smacked against a back foot, but failed to hold. This was too close. He had come out too early.

The wall loomed ahead of him, the top just out of reach. Lhai knew he couldn't risk another dive down into the bailey. This was his last chance. He held his breath and gave his wings one last desperate push. He did not fly, unfettered, over the edge as he had so often dreamt. Instead, he came up just short, but managed to reach out and grab the top of the wall with his front talons. Gasping for breath, every muscle in his body burning, he pulled up and threw himself over, to the outside.

By sheer coincidence, he had climbed up and over the wall furthest from the main gate, which only now was being opened to allow his pursuers out. Lhai took a deep breath and glided toward the nearby wood, trying to recover his strength. He knew there was no catching him now. He picked up his wings again and began to beat them in a slow consistent rhythm, powering out over the treetops. He was free.

~~~~~

Lhai circled high overhead, riding the gusts of warm air rising from the fires below. He wove his way around the tall columns of black smoke, trying to see what he could.

Lord Ziaud had been all too happy to receive him, given that Lhai had provided useful intelligence to Ziaud's father many years ago. But Lhai was quick to assure Ziaud this was not a business dealing. He was no spy. This was personal. Ziaud agreed to give Lhai safe passage in out and out of his castle, for the price of information. Over a long meal of finely roasted goat, Lhai had told him all he knew and heard about Lord Kala's defenses. He told him about the number of fighters in the company, how poorly led they were, and how easily frightened. And he told Ziaud about the walls and of the weak spots near his hiding place.

Ziaud needed no convincing of Lhai's story of confinement. "Kala always had held symbolism over strength, like those gold painted spears," he said. "Just like him to find a dragon and put it in shackles."

Armed with Lhai's information, Ziaud needed little prodding to attack Kala. He had wanted to do so for years, but didn't know enough of the details of Kala's company to be certain of victory. Ziaud was a conservative man, but one who would strike when the opportunity arose.

Lhai had given only one condition to Ziaud before he told all he knew. "There is a boy," he said, "named Lessard. He is the one who helped me."

"You want to ensure he is not hurt?" Ziaud asked.

"More than that," Lhai said. "He has no real family. After you finish with Kala, I doubt he will have anything left at all. Take him in. Give him a home. He will do right by you, I think."

Ziaud weighed the condition for a few moments.

"But under no circumstances are you to keep him prisoner," Lhai added.

"Very well," Ziaud said. "It is a small price to pay to be rid of Kala."

When the clang of steel on steel and the war cries of men in battle stopped, Lhai dropped slowly down toward Kala's castle. He alighted on the north wall, the one opposite the site of Ziaud's attack. The sounds of battle had given way to the sounds of grief and pain, of wounded men calling to the Maker for salvation, and of women weeping for those already gone. Ziaud's men gathered prisoners, marching small groups back and forth across the bailey.

Lhai could see that Kala was among them, bloodied from a gash above his eyes. His prophecy had come true. The dragon had left the bailey and Kala's rule had come crashing down.

Away from the prisoners, amongst a group of soldiers standing under Ziaud's banner, stood Lessard. He looked small and helpless compared to the soldiers, but Lhai knew better. He hung overhead until their eyes met.

Lhai had seen what he needed to see. He smiled and flew away toward the wood.

# The Mask

Jonah couldn't sleep. Not because he wasn't tired
– far from it. There was the long flight, followed by the
even-longer cab ride ("how is that even possible?" Jonah
wondered). Then three nightly sessions of "reuniting"
with Katherine. They'd missed each other terribly in three
weeks since she came to DC. Katherine, however, had no
problem going to sleep. Her head rested comfortably on
Jonah's shoulder, arm draped across his chest, her
breathing occasionally punctuated by an uneven snore.
Even the city had gone to sleep, as the lights of the DC
skyline had long since slipped into darkness.

For Jonah, the problem was not restlessness,
caffeine overdose, or the sugar drenched chocolate
explosion he and Katherine shared for dessert (although
that didn't help). What was keeping Jonah awake was the
mask. The mask that was inexplicably hung from the
archway that demarcated the bedroom from the rest of
Katherine's loft apartment. At first, Jonah didn't even
notice the mask, until Katherine pointed it out proudly
during a tour of her temporary home. It was to be part of
the exhibit at the Smithsonian Institution she was
working on, once anybody figured out what it was.
Katherine was so taken by it that she convinced the

curators to let her put it in the Institution-furnished apartment to better "study" it. She could study it equally well at her station in the Institution, of course. Katherine wanted it there simply because she thought it looked cool.

"Cool" was not the first word that sprang to Jonah's mind when he laid eyes on the mask. "Frightening" was more like it. So was "scary" and "seriously weird." One thing was clear - it involved snakes. Lots of snakes. Jonah hated snakes. He hated even more not being able to pinpoint the number of snakes involved; new ones seemed to spring up every time he looked at it. And now, as the mask glinted in the moonlight, some had disappeared. But Jonah knew they were still there and it freaked him out.

In fact, he'd been well and truly freaked ever since he laid eyes on the mask. That first night, after dinner at a nearby Ethiopian restaurant and a long stroll through the neighborhood, Jonah and Katherine retired to the bedroom to reunite. Katherine excused herself to change behind a screen, while Jonah climbed into bed. He fixated on the mask, wondering what sort of spirit possessed someone to make it. Was it a joke? The work of a lunatic? Laden with some deep religious meaning that Jonah's atheistic mind just couldn't grasp? He got so lost in these thoughts that he hadn't noticed Katherine emerge from behind the screen. It took a polite clearing of the throat from Katherine for Jonah to shift his gaze from the mask to her curvaceous frame and how seductively the new black silk negligee clung to her curves.

In a playfully disappointed tone, Katherine asked, "What on Earth, Jonah, could be more important right now than your sexy girlfriend whom you haven't seen in three weeks parading around in her underwear?"

"Sorry, honey, it's that mask. It just . . .," Jonah shuddered, "makes me nervous."

"Well, maybe I can take your mind off that mask for a while, huh?" Katherine said as she slid into bed and wrapped her arms around him.

The diversion that night, and the night after, and this night, too, had only been temporary. Eventually, during the night, Jonah rolled over, woke up, and found himself face to face with the mask. This night was like all the others.

As Jonah sat up and wondered about the mask, something else did draw his attention - a noise, like a metallic rattle, coming through the front door. Jonah changed the target of his stare and looked towards the door. Thanks to a combination of moonlight and the light from next door shining in through the kitchen, Jonah saw a crouched human form slowly creep into the apartment. As the form moved silently towards the living room and disappeared behind a divider, another sight caught Jonah's attention out of the corner of his right eye.

It was the mask. More specifically, it was the snakes in the mask. And they were moving. Slowly uncoiling from the mask, the snakes stretched forth like ghostly fingers into the night. If Jonah was freaked before, he was gripped with fright now. "First a break-in and now some kind of poltergeist? Holy shit!" Jonah thought.

Paralyzed with fear, Jonah watched as the snakes slowly turned around and dove underneath the mask, out under the archway. Jonah peered around the corner and saw the trail of snakes turn around the corner of a divider, where the intruder had gone. He heard something drop - something heavy, but not breakable - and heard the squeaky scurrying of tennis shoes on a bare wood floor. He saw the intruder fly out of the apartment, not even closing the door behind him. As Jonah struggled to process this turn of events, the snakes silently drifted back into the bedroom and settled back into the mask. Still freaked, but no longer completely frightened, Jonah got up, closed the door, and checked the lock and deadbolt. Then he went back to bed.

Katherine lay there, mouth slightly open, arms splayed across the pillows. She snored gently, oblivious to the world around her. Jonah slid in beside her, slipping himself underneath one arm. He looked at the mask and then, for the first time in three days, went to sleep.

# Jury Duty

Dent arrived at the courthouse early Monday morning, as ordered. The email had come just the week before, reminding him of an obligation he didn't know he had. Frantic digging through the piles of mail on his kitchen counter uncovered a more detailed notice from the District Court of the Southern District of West Virginia, postmarked six weeks ago. He had called to try and get out of it, but the shriveled old woman from the clerk's office on the video screen had said it was much too late.

He'd broken down and gone to talk to his brother-in-law, Russell, who was as sleazy and loophole knowledgeable as any attorney on Earth. It didn't help.

~~~~~

"Tell me how to get out of jury duty," Dent said.

Russell clicked his tongue and shook his head. "Sorry, friend, that's not possible. Not anymore."

"Seriously," Dent said, "I've got everything booked for Fiji. If I can't go now, the money's gone."

"Are the tickets transferrable?" Russell asked, grinning.

Dent gave him his best serious look. "Tell me how to get out of this."

"I really can't," Russell said. "Blame Congress for passing the Increasing Jury Service Act of 2052."

"The what?"

Russell rolled his eyes. "You know, if you had one of these, like most normal people," he said, tapping the G-K port just behind his right ear, "I could just dump the information into your brain for the next few days."

"But since that's not an option," Dent said.

"Why don't you have one?" Russell asked. For two decades, they had been used by tens of millions of people all over the country to download information into their short-term memory rather than writing it down. "I mean, your sister says it's just because you couldn't stand the thought of the pain, but that can't be it. Can it?"

"That's part of it," Dent said. "I mean, why do that if you don't have to? Why let someone cut into your head, just for the sake of convenience?"

"Yeah, but so many people have them now," Russell said. "You almost need one just to get along in life."

Dent shook his head. "That's not true. There are more people without ports than you realize, just because they're not likely to travel in your circles."

Russell wasn't giving up. "Don't you ever think how easy it would be to zap something into your mind? Just for a few days?"

"No," Dent said. "Besides, I'm a thoughtful, slower paced kind of guy. I don't mind reading. And I've found that most people don't mind indulging me."

Russell shrugged. "Your loss."

"Now, tell me about this jury duty act," Dent said, trying to get the conversation back on track."

Russell sighed. "You see, years ago, almost nobody actually served on juries. People could get off of jury duty if they had certain kinds of jobs, a family member they had to take care of. . . ."

"A planned and paid-for vacation," Dent interjected.

"Yes, exactly," Russell said, continuing perfectly in stride. "On top of that, lawyers would take hours and hours picking a jury – trying to find the 12 dumbest people in the room who they could mold to their view of the case. A lawyer could even kick somebody off a jury for no reason at all. As a result, lots of people got called for jury duty and then were excused before the trial started." Russell was obviously reveling in his quasi-expert status. "That didn't sit well with some people, of course. They saw jury duty as a great civic duty, like voting, and thought it shouldn't be so easily evaded. Others worried about whether defendants were actually getting 'juries of their peers' once everyone was weeded out by the system."

"So how does this affect me?" Dent asked, losing patience.

"Well, my friend, Congress sought to get rid of most of the loopholes that let people to skip jury service.

It was mostly the criminal defense people, at first. But eventually the civic duty people signed on and, voila, the Increasing Jury Service Act of 2052. Now you can only be excused from jury duty if you have some sort of impending medical disaster or if you know the defendant or one of the lawyers. Basically, it takes an act of God to get you out of jury duty these days."

"Shit," Dent said, slumping back in his chair, arms crossed.

"In return for all that, at least, you're guaranteed to only sit on one case and then you're done. And, once you've served, you can't be called back for ten years," Russell said.

It was little consolation. Dent got up and started to walk out of the office.

Just as Dent was to walk out the door, Russell said, "So, what about those tickets?"

~~~~~

Now Dent found himself in a large wood paneled room with dozens of others, none of whom looked like they wanted to be there. His flight had already left without him. His travel agent had mentioned later flights that day as an alternative, but Dent told him that wouldn't be good enough.

He scanned through the morning news on his phone, waiting for something to happen. He noticed that some of the others had phones or tablets plugged into their G-K ports, getting the morning's news dumped directly into their brains. Dent rolled his eyes, thankful again that he'd never gone in for that nonsense.

Shortly, a round little woman entered and explained that the assembled throng would be divided up and sent to different courtrooms to start their service. Dent's name was called, and he followed about a dozen others to the courtroom of the Honorable Benjamin E. Gholar, III.

Dent flopped down in the first open seat in the jury box, forcing several others to climb over him. Two heavy wooden tables were set up parallel to the judge's bench, perpendicular to the jury box. Based on earlier conversations with Russell, the nearest table would belong to the prosecutors, the Assistant United States Attorneys. Which left the far table for the defense, most likely public defenders, assuming it was a criminal case.

There were two defense lawyers. One was an older woman who moved with a precision and calmness that suggested years of experience, while the young man on the other side of the table shifted nervously. Between them was another young man, presumably the defendant, wearing a suit that was clearly not his, as it was a little too big for his slender frame, like a little boy wearing his father's Sunday best. When the jurors came in he cast a quick glance at each, but looked away if anyone tried to make eye contact. Dent wondered what he might have done, but quickly put such questions out of his mind.

Without any signal that Dent could hear, people took their seats. One woman, sitting at a desk near the foot of the judge's bench, rose and announced the entry of Judge Gholar. With a precision that could only come from practice, everyone else in the courtroom rose as the judge took the bench. The jurors followed suit, after a delay of recognition at the proper procedure. Everyone sat at his command. Dent obliged the convention, but without enthusiasm. One of the court security officers gave him a stern look.

Judge Gholar introduced himself and told them about the nature of the case. Dent had guessed right. The young man in the ill-fitting suit, named Byron Davison, was charged with a crime – distribution of rapture, the hot new party drug that was sending unsuspecting college kids to the hospital. The judge also identified the attorneys who were involved, confirming Dent's suspicions that they were AUSAs and public defenders. Somewhat smug in his ability to suss all this out, Dent sat back in his chair as Judge Gholar continued his remarks.

"Now, in a moment I am going to ask you, as a group, a series of questions to determine whether you may serve on this jury. Before I do that, however, I want to emphasize one thing that you all must remember during your service in this case or, indeed, any other criminal case." Dent noticed that the judge had been reading from a script up to this point, but now he lifted his gaze and fixed it directly on the jurors. "Mr. Davison enters this court today behind a firewall of innocence. He has to prove nothing in order to walk out of this room a free man. Instead, the Government must breach that firewall by proving, beyond a reasonable doubt, that Mr. Davison committed the offense with which he is charged." Judge Gholar paused for a moment and then said, in much the same voice he must use to discipline his dogs, "Never forget that."

With the jury sufficiently admonished, the judge returned to his script and began asking questions of the jurors, seeking some response if anything was amiss. Dent was amused at most of them. Do you all reside in the Southern District of West Virginia, Charleston Division? Have any of you been previously convicted of a felony? As if the court wouldn't know. Does anyone know any of the attorneys involved in this case, the defendant, or the judge? After each question, the judge would look up briefly and, hearing no discouraging word, continue to the next.

Judge Gholar's next question broke the rhythm a bit. "I want to ask a question that is not about your duty as jurors, but how we will proceed with the trial itself." After a pause to turn the page, the judge asked, "Is there anyone here who does not have a G-K implant compliant with SCIP version 3.1.4.03?"

Dent's ears perked up at the mention of the implant, surprised to hear them mentioned. He raised his hand.

But a raised hand was apparently not in Judge Gholar's script, as he began another question. Dent let out an exaggerated cough that was loud enough to bring things to a halt. The security officer shot him another scowl, but Dent didn't care. He had a question and he needed an answer." Your Honor?"

The judge raised his eyes from his script and focused on Dent." Yes, juror number 11 . . . Mr. Dent, is it?"

"Yes, Your Honor."

"You are not compliant with SCIP version 3.1.4.03? I don't think that's a problem; we'll just have to dig out some older equipment. Jerry . . . ," the judge said as he turned to one of his numerous underlings.

"No, Your Honor," Dent said, interrupting without care." It's not that I'm behind on the updates. I don't have a G-K implant at all."

He heard audible gasps from around the court. There were only two spectators in the gallery, but Dent was sure they were both stunned. He noticed one of them tapping furiously on a tablet, recording the oddity for some sort of posterity. Out-of-date implants were one thing, but living without one completely? It was unthinkable to most people.

Judge Gholar looked confused for a moment—a judicial deer caught in the headlights. Once he found his footing, he continued. "Members of the jury, I need to discuss something with the attorneys in this case and Mr. Davison. This should only take a few minutes."

With that, Dent heard a "thwip" and the jury box was encased in a field of some kind. Dent watched as the lawyers erupted into pantomime argument, like in a silent movie. All the jurors could hear were each other.

"What is he, a Quaker?" Dent heard from over his right shoulder. He turned quickly and caught his fellow juror by surprise. He was a large older man who clearly thought that Dent would not overhear his remark. His expression was one of surprise and embarrassment at being caught by the target of his barb.

Dent wasted no time firing back. "I believe you're thinking of the Amish," he said, looking the man straight in the eyes. "Quakers are quite technologically literate. It's the Amish that ride in buggies and shun electricity and such. Either way, to answer your question, I'm neither Quaker nor Amish. I'm a Yakovist. Have you heard the Yet Again Another Testament of Jesus Christ?" With that, Dent turned back around in his seat. He wasn't, in fact, a Yakovist, but he knew that the sect was so misunderstood, particularly in this area, that it was an easy and instant way to make someone else feel uncomfortable. This whole process had been a great discomfort to Dent. Why shouldn't someone else share in it?

"I don't know how you survive without one," asked the woman, middle aged with wispy brown hair, seated beside him. "I use mine all the time. Helps me keep my to-do list straight." "I'm not a Luddite," Dent said. "I just don't see the point of letting someone inside my head so I don't have to write down a shopping list. I mean, have you ever seen a G-K operation? They have to cut your skull open, install the jack, and then wire it into your brain. It's one thing to do that to cure somebody who's sick, but just for convenience? No thanks." Dent waved away the idea with his hand.

Dent heard the "thwip" again and noticed the ambient sounds of the large courtroom swirl in his ears before Judge Gholar could speak. "Members of the jury, I'm afraid this may take a little while longer. I beg your indulgence." The judge then trained his gaze on Dent. "Mr. Dent, could you please step down out of the jury box?"

Dent did as the judge asked. As he stepped down toward the prosecution table, he heard the "thwip" behind him.

"Mr. Dent. You've presented us with a little bit of a dilemma. You see, when G-K implants became very popular, it was natural that they would find their way into our proceedings. About five years ago, this court began experimenting with using short-term memory flashes as a means of presenting evidence. It's much quicker, as you probably know, to simply upload a chunk of information rather than have it presented as testimony in court."

Dent nodded, even though he'd never been in any kind of court before and didn't have any real idea of how things worked, beyond streaming dramas he'd seen on the Net.

"At first," Judge Gholar said, "the only information for which this process was used was uncontested facts—things that both parties could agree on. But, eventually, the efficiencies became too great and it was hard to ignore the possibility of dumping all of the relevant information into the jury's short-term memory. All of what most people think of as a 'trial'— witness testimony, cross examination, exhibits--are done in advance by the parties. The attorneys, with Mr. Davison's input, of course, assemble and question witnesses on video and we resolve any sort of objections then and there. When the jury receives the evidence, they don't have to worry about interruptions, putting improperly admitted evidence out of their minds, etc. Days of trial are compressed into minutes. Jury deliberations aren't any faster, of course, but when the rest of the trial lasts one hour at most, it's quite easy to allow the jury to take their time."

Dent got some idea of where this might be going. He was out of place in a modern high-tech courtroom.

"Obviously, this system only works if everyone on the jury has a G-K implant. You are . . . well, quite frankly, you're a bit of an original around here, Mr. Dent. You're the first person I've had in my courtroom who lacked a G-K implant since we started running trials this way. You see my dilemma, I'm sure."

Dent found an opening and struck. "No, Your Honor, I don't see the dilemma," he said. "I was required to be here by law. No exceptions, that's what I was told. Nobody told me about G-K implants or SCIP protocols." He didn't mention his blown vacation. It seemed a bridge too far, at this point. As Dent spoke, he cast a glance at the defense table and Davison. The defendant appeared somewhat heartened by this turn of events. Anything to put off the inevitable, perhaps?

At this point, a voice came from the prosecution table. "Mr. Dent, it appears that you are familiar with the 2052 Jury Act." The other AUSA, whose chair was empty when Dent was figuring out all the players, was standing and addressing him. He looked cool and composed as he began his cross examination.

"Yes, I'm somewhat familiar with it," Dent said.

"What many people don't realize," the AUSA continued, "is that even as strict as the Act is, there are ways to allow a person to be excused from jury service."

"I know: direct bias against one of the parties or serious impending medical catastrophe," Dent shot back. He turned to Judge Gholar. "Your Honor, I've never met any of these people in my life and I'm healthy as an ox. Those don't apply to me."

The judge sat silent as the AUSA continued. "Yes, Mr. Dent, but there is another provision. Section 17(a)(2) of the Act says that if any person reports for jury duty and is for any reason unable to participate in the jury's reception of evidence or instructions or take part in the jury's deliberations, he may request that he be excused from the case." The AUSA finished his recitation, smiling smugly at his apparently foolproof means of keeping Dent from throwing their well-oiled train off the tracks.

"So, Mr. Dent," Judge Gholar chimed in, "the decision is really up to you. You are, technically, unable to participate in the reception of evidence and argument in this case in the same fashion as your fellow jury members. If you wish, you may be excused."

Dent only now noticed that his fists were clenched, his fingernails digging into the skin of his palm. He tried to calm his racing heart by taking a few deep breaths while he looked at the oversized ceremonial clock on the opposite wall. If he was excused now, he could probably make one of those later flights his travel agent had mentioned. It wasn't even about Fiji any more. Was he somehow deficient? A lesser member of society because he hadn't been cut on and "upgraded" like most of the rest of the citizenry? Forget Fiji. It would be there next year.

"I'm sorry, Your Honor, but I don't understand. I'm a reasonably intelligent human being. I can understand English, speak it fairly well, can remember things that are told or shown to me. I'm capable of listening to Your Honor's instructions and the arguments of counsel and rendering a verdict. I . . . I just don't see how my lack of an implant keeps me from acting like a juror." As he finished, Dent looked back at the AUSA. He was clearly not expecting Dent to take the high road. Dent could see the sweat start to break on his forehead. He pressed on. "What if I don't request to be removed from the jury?"

Judge Gholar thought for a second before answering. "Well, I suppose we would have to go forward with the old trial procedure. The parties would present witnesses and other evidence, I would give instructions on the offense charged against Mr. Davison, the attorneys would make final arguments, and the jury would deliberate."

Dent now realized why the AUSA was so nervous. For years, none of them had to go through the rigor of a live trial. They hadn't actually tried any cases. They did everything in advance, no doubt with multiple takes to ensure maximum persuasive power. The attorneys were used to acting in movies, and Dent was threatening to make them step up on the live stage once again. That clinched it.

At this point, one of the public defenders—the older woman—

stood up. "Your Honor, if I could be heard very briefly. Mr. Davison has absolutely no objection to going forward with a trial in the classic sense, if I may use that term. He has put a great deal on the line here by pleading not guilty to these charges and would object to any action by the Court or coercion by the Government that would cause a fit and able juror to give up his right to sit on this jury. Thank you."

Dent was buoyed by the support from defense counsel. "In that case, Your Honor," Dent concluded, "I wish to stay on this jury and hear Mr. Davison's case."

"But . . . Your Honor!"

Dent heard another gasp from behind him, from the AUSA, as he impotently protested.

"I'm sorry, Mr. Ross, but it's Mr. Dent's decision to make. Do the parties need a few minutes to prepare?"

Both sides answered with a fairly meek, "Yes, Your Honor," punctuated with a barely audible "Please, dear God."

"Very well," Judge Gholar said. Dent heard another "thwip" as the cone of silence over the jury box dissipated. "Members of the jury, we will take a brief recess before the parties begin the presentation of their cases." He didn't mention anything about the change in proceedings. Dent returned to his seat, suppressing a smile and reveling in his victory.

The brief recess lasted almost an hour, and when court was called to order there was a different AUSA in place of the one with whom Dent had sparred. This one was older, with visible lines on his face. He had done this before, in the good old days, Dent was certain.

As the jurors settled in, Judge Gholar read the indictment against Davison and called upon the Government to make their opening statement. The new AUSA stood up and walked slowly to the lectern and faced the jury. "May it please the court," he said, slowly, voice trembling.

Dent simply sat back, listened, and smiled.

~~~~~

The trial took the rest of that day, all of the next, and part of the following morning. It was not a particularly compelling case. In fact, Dent was quite disappointed when all was said and done. Davison was very, very guilty, caught on video selling a large amount of rapture to an undercover police officer. The video was crystal clear and, at one point, Davison looked right into the camera, like he wanted to make sure they got his good side. Dent gave him as much of the benefit of the doubt as he could, but he had to convict. Deliberations took less than an hour.

When the verdict was in and Davison had been taken away, Dent wandered out to the lobby, only to turn and come face to face with Davison's attorneys.

"Mr. Dent," the older woman said, holding out a hand. "Thank you for standing up."

"Me?" Dent asked. "Didn't do your client much good in the end."

"Perhaps not. But it's been a long time since we've had a trial like that, a real trial. My young friend here had never seen one." She nodded toward the young man standing behind her, clutching a stack of papers.

"You're welcome, then, I guess," Dent said. "But why go through with it at all? Your guy was obviously guilty, if you don't mind me saying."

She smiled. "Mr. Dent, as the defense attorney there are lots of decisions I get to make. But whether to go to trial? That's a decision that's up to my client. Doesn't matter what I think." She shrugged and Dent caught the subtext of what she was saying.

"Yeah, well, sorry I couldn't do more," he said.

"You did what you could," she said." Sometimes, you just have to lie down in front of the bulldozer, right?"

"Er, I guess?" Dent didn't get the reference.

~~~~~

A week after the trial, Dent finally got around to watching and reading the news coverage of the Davison case. The trial had been covered just due to the fact that there was a trial at all, not because of how it turned out.

When word leaked out to the media that someone was actually going on trial, with witnesses and all, the spectator gallery in the courtroom filled to capacity. Only the one reporter who had been there from the beginning knew why, and it gave her an exclusive that she beat to death over the next two days.

After the trial was over, the media poked and prodded the jurors. Dent didn't answer questions, but the others were more than happy to, once they realized that Dent caused them to be locked into trial for three days instead of two hours. They were not pleased. The man who made the Quaker remark wondered, on many different media outlets, whether Dent was some sort of radical, using the trial to force society to step back into the Stone Age.

Dent didn't think of it that way, of course. He was forced to be there and simply didn't want it to come to nothing. If there were side effects of his little stunt, all the better. Russell called once the trial was over, asking if Dent needed any representation should he try to sell the rights to his story. Dent politely refused. There was nothing to sell. There was no great story there.

But Dent did know one thing. He was free from the specter of jury duty for at least ten years. And he was already planning a way to get to Fiji.

# The Missing Legion

Taiman hadn't anticipated this. The army camp stretched across most of the open ground between the deep forest of the Arbor and the slowly flowing current of the Water Road. It would have been foolish for him to try and slip past.

"Halt!" called out one of the sentries at the edge of the camp. The other two aimed their muskets at Taiman, looking as if they desperately wanted to use them.

Taiman did as he was told, bringing his horse to a stop and raising his hands. "I want no trouble."

The one who appeared to be in charge wore a uniform of deep green to match the dense forests of the Arbor, not to mention his skin. The white and grey piping on the cuffs and collars meant he was from Durlandala. He was a corporal, based on the insignia on his shoulders. "Identify yourself."

"Taiman Innis of the Guild of Hunters," he said, slowly and clearly. "I want no part of your business. I only need to pass by."

"Just on maneuvers," said one of the others, a little defensively. The corporal shot him a quick look to keep him from saying anything more. Perhaps the eternal clashes between the cities of the Arbor were about to flare up once again.

"What's your business here, Guildsman?" the corporal asked.

"Tracking a great red wood ape," Taiman said. "It's gone into these woods, I'm certain. You can check my papers."

The corporal nodded. "Papers?"

Taiman pulled a sheet of paper from his saddlebag and held it out for the corporal. He took it then stepped back quickly. When it was clear the corporal could not read it, Taiman said, "That is my Guild certification. It says I am a hunter by profession and training. Check my weapons, if you have any doubt. They are not suitable for your work."

The corporal motioned for Taiman to dismount, which he did. Then the corporal stepped over to Taiman's horse and inspected the neatly packed weapons. He passed quickly over the long rifle and the cache of knives, but stopped when he found the bow and quiver. "What's this?"

"Neldathi short bow," Taiman said. "Bought it on a trip to Port Orford, down south. Ever been there?"

The corporal shook his head.

"Never seen anything like it. A city full of Altrerian traders, sailors from the Slaisal Islands, and looming over all of them are clutches of Neldathi wandering around. Ever seen one in person?"

"In a zoo!" cracked one of the others, which prompted laughter from them, but not the corporal.

"I don't mean those poor souls," Taiman said, turning to the other soldiers. "I'm talking about real Neldathi in their own land. Two feet taller than any of you, blue all over, and those long braids with the clan colors hanging down their backs. "Quite a sight." He shifted his attention back to the corporal. "And they are skilled craftsmen. If I need a bow, I want a Neldathi one."

The corporal turned away and motioned for Taiman to get back on his horse. "You're heading into the woods, you say?"

"Yes," Taiman said.

"Are you sure you want to do that?"

"Absolutely," Taiman said. "I've been chasing that beast for five days. If I can corner it in the woods, perhaps I can catch it alive."

"Will that be worth it, you think?" the corporal asked.

"Of course," Taiman said. "Why? You're not going to try and keep me from going, are you? Thought men in the Arbor valued free movement more than anything."

"We will not stop you," the corporal said. "But I would advise against going in, particularly if you don't know the area. It's very easy to get lost. Plus, they say things happen in those woods at night. Strange things, when the moons are full."

Taiman chuckled and sighed. "Thank you for the warning. Someday, the enlightenment that has come to the Guildlands will filter down to the Arbor as well. We no longer believe in superstitious nonsense. There are no strange things, only things that we do not understand. Besides, I am capable of handling any creature or person I might encounter. Now, if I may be on my way?"

The corporal told him how to best make his way around the camp and Taiman set off. He cursed the delay, but knew it had not spoiled his hunt. The beast had outrun him the day before, vanished from sight, but Taiman had held onto the trail. Barely.

His hopes rekindled when he spotted the beast through a telescope as it loped out of the trees in search of water. Once again he had a target to pursue. Taiman spurred his horse and charged off down river.

He did not take the beast by surprise. The noise, either from the camp whooping at Taiman's departure or the thunder of his horse's hooves caught its attention. Taiman pulled an arrow from the quiver on his horse's flank and drew the bow string tight. The beast was twice as large as Taiman, significantly bigger even than the tallest Neldathi he'd ever seen. Uglier too, covered in reddish brown fur from head to toe. The beast raised its head and caught Taiman's eyes just as he was ready to loose the arrow. It raced for the tree line, but not before Taiman let fly. The arrowhead struck its target in the back just below the left shoulder blade, but the beast continued to run into the forest, as if it had merely been bitten by a fly.

Taiman drove his horse on and followed the beast. The corporal had not been wrong about the woods, which quickly engulfed him. His horse struggled through the brush, stumbling over roots and vines. Taiman did his best to dodge the limbs that swung into his path, but rarely succeeded. He held on tight to the reins to keep from being knocked to the ground. The beast, more at home amongst the trees, moved with a lightness, grace, and speed that belied its size. Before long, it was out of sight. Again.

Taiman was lost and exhausted. Darkness was falling, with trees and clouds blocking most of what should have been full, silvery moons. The little moonlight there was reflected off something several dozen yards ahead of him. Hopefully it was the Water Road; at least then he would know where he was. Taiman dismounted and led his horse slowly through the trees.

It was not the Water Road. It was a lake, narrow and long, disappearing into the night. It would at least make a suitable place for a camp. Tomorrow, when the sun rose, he could find his way out of the forest. All there was to do tonight was to build a fire, find something to eat, and sleep very soundly.

Taiman chose a spot near the shore to serve as a campsite, with enough bare ground to stretch out without a root poking his back. As his horse slurped water from the lake, Taiman tried to summon the patience to catch a fish, but could not. Instead, he splashed some of the cold clear water onto his face, to wash away the grit of another fruitless day. Then he tied his horse to a nearby tree, sat down in front of the fire, and ate a bit of salted beef and stale bread from his pack. Slowly, the sky began to clear. Soon the full moons blazed brilliantly overhead. With his stomach at least calm, if not full, Taiman unrolled his blanket and lay down next to the fire.

~~~~~

Sleep came easily, but it did not last long. In the middle of the night, a nervous whinny from his horse woke Taiman. He opened his eyes and looked at his horse, which was staring over top of Taiman and behind him, towards the fire. Taiman rubbed his eyes and rolled over. There was a man on the other side of the fire, squatting on his haunches, studying him.

The man across the fire was white, almost glowing. He had the slight and short build of an Altrerian. However, in the light of the moons and the man's own aura, Taiman did not see even a hint of green in the man's skin. His eyes were the same pale white, with just a hint of black in the center. He looked like a soldier, but not from a modern army. He wore a suit of thin, white armor, rather than the standard uniforms of the day. Instead of a musket, he held a pike that was longer than either man was tall, with a barbed point at the end.

At first, Taiman was too surprised to be afraid. He could only manage to feebly ask, "Who are you?"

"Leave this place," the man replied, barely above a whisper.

"What?" Taiman asked. "Why? Who are you?"

"Leave this place," the man said in a calm measured tone. "What happens here is not for your eyes."

Taiman sat up, rubbing his eyes again, unsure whether this was a dream. "Why don't you tell me who you are before you start ordering me around? Who are you to tell me what I can see?"

Again the man replied, "Leave this place."

"Why should I?" Taiman asked, annoyed. "Always heard that all men are free in the Arbor, outside the city walls. That's what your people say in the Guildlands, at least. My friends and I always thought it was just propaganda and apparently we were right. Who are you to tell me to leave?"

There was no reply. In the silence, Taiman's annoyance gradually shifted towards alarm. He slid his right hand behind his back slowly, searching for the belt he took off just before he went to sleep. He searched for the handle of one of the knives that dangled from it. "It has been a long day, and only the last of several," he said as his fingers found a knife, wrapped around the hilt, and carefully slid it from its scabbard. "All I want is to get some sleep and find my way out of here when the sun comes up. Don't want any trouble."

"Leave this place," the man repeated. "Now."

Before Taiman could respond, a blur of light, in the corner of his eye, caught his attention. He looked to his right, down the shore, and saw another man, also all in white, standing on the edge of water. He was not carrying a long spear, like the man across the fire, but Taiman could tell he was wearing the same kind of armor. In his hands, he held a helmet with a large triangular plume on top. Taiman stared back at the man across the fire, at a loss for words.

"Leave this place," the man said again, the volume of his voice rising.

Even though the night air was crisp and cool, Taiman felt sweat rise up on his forehead. His heart racing, he gripped the knife tightly. "What do you mean? What's happening here? Who are you?"

The man stood and roared, "What happens here is not for your eyes!"

Instinct took over, and Taiman threw the knife. It was a perfect throw, the product of hours of practice and countless successful hunts. It should have buried itself deep in the other man's neck, just above the top of his breastplate. Instead, it flew straight through him and landed with a thud in the dirt behind. Taiman stared at the man for a moment, then back to the one standing on the shore. It was then that he saw a brilliant white light begin to filter up through the surface of the lake.

"Leave this place!" the man across the fire shouted, his voice ringing in Taiman's ears like thunder.

"I will not!" Taiman yelled back. "This is all in my head, some kind of dream. Perhaps there was some mold in that bread I ate and it's doing something to my mind. But you are not real. None of this is real!"

The man nodded. "You have made your choice," he said, then turned and began walking toward the shore.

Taiman quickly put on his boots, picked up the knife, and dashed to the tree where his horse was tied.

The horse was snorting and fidgeting, the white glow from the two apparitions dancing across its black eyes. Taiman stroked its muzzle to try and calm him.

When Taiman turned back to face the lake, the man from across the fire was standing there beside it, resting on his spear. The man on the shore had not moved. It looked like he was trying to get away from the water, to run into the trees, but could not. It was as if his feet were stuck in solid rock. A powerful white glow began to pulse in the lake, accompanied by the sound of stamping feet. It sounded as if a hundred men were marching in lock step down the street of any city. But there were no streets here.

The first rank emerged from the surface of the lake, ten men, ramrod straight, with long spears like the one held by the man across the fire. All were white as alabaster. From where Taiman stood they appeared to blend into one illuminated mass. They marched up from the water towards the man on the shore. First one rank came, then another and another. When the fifth row emerged from the water, the man from across the fire joined them, filling in at the end nearest to Taiman's campfire. Ten rows in all emerged from the water that remained still as glass.

Taiman didn't know what he was seeing, but it was marvelous. It was calm, stately, almost solemn. Was this really all a dream? Was he still safely asleep beside the fire on the lake shore? The sweat trickling down his neck told him otherwise. He gripped the knife tightly in his hand even though he knew using it would be futile.

Next came the sounds, the wails. Shrieks of pain and agony, like the siren call of a wounded bird of prey, fending off the carrion eaters by sheer force of will. The column moved as one, endowed with a singular purpose, a mass of blurry white light, towards the man on the shore, but the noise was cacophonous, random, and vicious. Taiman covered his ears, but it did no good.

When the first row of the column was about to reach the man on the shore, they lowered their spears to point at him. Only then could Taiman make out words amidst the din. They came from the man on the shore, who was screaming. "No! You can't do this! I am not responsible! It was not my fault! I am not to blame! No!"

With the last row of the column now out of the water, all order broke down, and the mass of soldiers charged at the man on the shore, shrieking howls of rage. The protests of the man on the shore were drowned out as they set upon him with spears, swords, and bare hands. The individual soldiers, and their target, became one as the scene turned into one immense white fireball on the shore of the lake. The wails grew louder until Taiman thought his head would explode. He watched, hands over his ears, as the ball grew and grew until it shattered brilliantly against the night sky in an eruption of pure light.

Then it was quiet. When the white spots faded from Taiman's eyes, he saw that the column had reassembled. It was marching back into the lake, under the water, accompanied only by the sound of marching feet. The further out the column went, the more the men struggled, the weight of their armor and weapons dragging them down into the water. The man from across the fire stood on the shore overseeing the maneuver. Without warning, he turned and fixed his gaze on Taiman. "What happens here is not for your eyes," he roared, with a fury amplified even beyond his original commands. "Leave this place!"

There was another bright light.

~~~~~

When Taiman awoke it was dark. He heard voices, familiar but not necessarily friendly, walking around him and talking softly. It was the soldiers from the camp, the ones who had detained him. Why was it so dark? What happened to the moons? To his campfire? "Where am I?" he asked, hoping for an answer from anyone. "Is it still night? Have you no lanterns or torches?"

"I was afraid of that," he heard the corporal say, but not in response to him. The voice got closer, as if it was walking towards Taiman, and explained, calmly if not kindly, "You're at the Durlan army camp, along the Water Road. It's mid-morning."

"What?" Taiman said, bolting upright with a splitting pain in his head. He reached for his face and felt to see if had had been blindfolded or masked. He felt only his eyes. They were open, yet he could see only darkness. "What happened?"

"We were going to ask you," a second voice said. "After you galloped off on your hunt yesterday, we thought we wouldn't see you again. Then this morning, we found you, unconscious, lying along the river. Your horse was circling around, but appears unhurt. Naturally, we thought the beast must have put up a fight, but . . . ." The voice trailed off, not knowing how to finish. "What happened to you?"

Taiman lay back down, and the pain in his head subsided slightly. It all came back to him—the man across the fire, the man on the shore, the marching column. And the noise. The horrible, ear-splitting noise. He told the soldiers all he could remember.

When he was finished, the corporal spoke again. "It's the missing legion," he said. No one else in the tent said a word. "I'm sure of it."

"That's preposterous," the second voice said.

"What's the missing legion?" Taiman asked, ignoring the second voice.

"Nothing more than a legend," answered a third voice, one that sounded confident and certain, a voice of command. "Hundreds of years ago, Tomondala and Maladondala fought a war that lasted decades. Their armies roamed across this part of the Arbor for years. The Tomons were famous for the fierce loyalty and bravery of their common foot soldiers. When others broke and ran, the Tomons stood and fought, to the last man if those were their orders."

"So?" Taiman interrupted. "How does that lead to me being blind?"

The storyteller continued, undaunted. "During one battle, a legion led by a young commander of noble birth, one who had no business actually leading men, was separated from the rest of the army and pinned down by a Maladon force. The commander ordered his legion to fall back to the shore of a lake and hold that position at all cost. His men knew it was a mistake. With the water at their back, they would have no way to retreat. The commander insisted, however, and the men did as they were told. They fought bravely, but the Maladons were too strong, too numerous, and they drove the Tomons into the lake. The entire legion was wiped out. A hundred men dead. Only the commander survived. He climbed a tree and hid until the sun went down and the Maladons were gone."

"But that's just a story children tell around a campfire to scare each other," said the second voice. "Who would be so foolish?"

The storyteller stammered slightly before continuing. "I'm just telling it the way I heard it. All history knows is that the legion was lost. Nobody really knows what happened to it."

"But," Taiman prodded.

"But," the corporal said, pausing for a moment, "the legend says the ghosts of the legion rose up and killed their commander in revenge, their souls no longer bound by the same code of loyalty. The story goes that some nights, when the moons are full, the legion and its commander act out this revenge. But, it is only a story, right?"

Taiman took a long moment to think, then raised his hands in front of his face, desperate to see something, anything. "I cannot say, corporal," he said, finally, "but I know what I saw.  Spent my life hunting the most dangerous creatures of this land. None of it prepared me for what happened last night."

"Are you saying you believe in 'strange things' now, Guildsman?" asked someone else.

Taiman knew the truth, knew what he had seen with his own eyes, but he could not bring himself to answer the question.

# Fine Print

A small young man was standing on the front stoop, clearly still in his twenties but mostly bald nonetheless. Beads of sweat danced across his forehead. A white pen stood out like a signal flare in the pocket of his immaculately pressed black shirt. He was looking at a clipboard when Gillian opened the door. It startled him.

"I'm sorry," she said, wiping perspiration away from her eyes.

"Just caught me a bit off guard, ma'am. I was beginning to think no one was home."

"I dozed off for a bit." Should have stayed on the couch, Gillian thought. "Can I help you?"

"Yes, ma'am," he said, taking one last look at the clipboard. "Are you the lady of the house?"

Gillian chuckled. He was working from a script, one that needed some updating. "I am *a* lady of the house, yes," she said with a slight smile. It confused him. "My wife took our daughters to soccer practice," she explained, bailing him out. "I have purchasing authority for this home, if that's what you're asking."

"Yes, ma'am," he answered with a slight quiver in his voice. "Thank you." He took a deep breath and launched back into his script. "My name is Kai and I work for Infinity Energy Services." He shifted slightly to one side.

Gillian noticed the small black van parked in the street in front of the house. On the side was a large symbol for infinity in blazing yellow. Underneath, in block letters, it read, "all your power needs for all of time."

Kai continued. "If I could have just a few minutes of your day, ma'am, I'd like to tell you about an exciting new product that could change your life – and the life of your family – forever."

"Are you from the power company?" Gillian asked.

"No, ma'am, I am not an employee or representative of Vandalia Power Supply or any of its subsidiaries." A pause, then back to the script. "Would you be interested in hearing about the products Infinity has to offer?"

Gillian's urge was to close the door in Kai's face and return to her nap. But it's not every day someone comes along offering to sell you power. Kai looked harmless enough. Besides, the power bill was the largest they had, aside from the mortgage. She was interested in anything that might bring that down. "Sure, why not? Come in," she said, stepping back to allow him through the door.

She led him inside and gestured toward the kitchen table. It was covered with the kids' homework, but she quickly cleared a spot for Kai to set down his clipboard. "Have a seat. And my name is Gillian, by the way. Could I get you a cold glass of water?"

"Yes, ma'am. Thank you," he answered.

As she filled a pair of glasses with ice and water, Gillian said, "The heat's really been something this past week, huh?"

"Yes, ma'am," he answered. "Has your neighborhood been hit by the blackouts? The heat is really taking a toll on the grid."

"We've had a few," she said, filling a glass from the tap. "More brownouts around here, though. Not as bad, but not good, you know?" She handed Kai a glass and sat down across the table from him.

"Thanks," he said, taking a quick sip. "Can I assume, ma'am, that based on what you just said, your current energy needs aren't being completely met?"

Gillian fanned herself with her hand without giving it much thought. "Is it that bad in here?"

"Not so bad as I've felt in other places. But it appears that either your air conditioning system needs to be serviced or there isn't enough power to run it at full capacity."

Gillian nodded. "It's only running at about sixty percent." Because that's all we can afford, she kept herself from saying.

"Do you get your energy only from Vandalia via the grid?"

"Vandalia installed some solar panels a few years ago, but they're only good for so much," she answered.

"You said you had more brownouts than blackouts," he said. "When was the last time you had a problem?"

"Last week was the latest one, I think."

"And how often do they happen, ma'am?"

"Two or three times a month, maybe once a week in the middle of summer." It sounded worse when she said it out loud. When she was growing up, brownouts were unheard of and blackouts were rare, limited to the aftermath of thunderstorms. They had become such a regular part of life in the past few years as the temperatures rose that she never really thought about them anymore.

The power drops themselves weren't the worst of it. They were paying out the nose for electricity, even when the solar panels were working. It had put a strain on them, especially since Bianca's firm started cutting back. Gillian's clients were fewer and farther between, as well. Arguing about the power bill was a regular flashpoint between them.

"What if I told you that Infinity Energy Services could make those problems a thing of the past?" His voice changed tone, as if he'd moved past the awkward information gathering phase and was into more familiar pitch territory.

"I'd say that sounds too good to be true."

He laughed. "To be honest, ma'am, if I didn't work for Infinity and didn't have one of our products at home, I'd be very suspicious as well."

Gillian took a long drink of water. "I appreciate your honesty. What kind of products?"

Kai looked like a fisherman who just got a big one to bite. It was time to reel her in. "Infinity specializes in alternative energy generation systems – AEGs, for short. An AEG is a simple device that attaches to your home's electrical system and provides a consistent supply of power at low cost. You can use an AEG as a supplement to other power sources or you can let Infinity take care of all your energy needs for one low monthly rate."

"Uh huh," Gillian said. "What's the catch?" Gillian knew there had to be a catch somewhere and she was damned sure not going to let him glide over it.

"No catch, ma'am. Just inexpensive, plentiful, trouble-free power," Kai answered with the polished precision of a trained salesman.

"How does it work?"

"Well, the main unit goes in the garage or basement, near the circuit breaker. Our technicians would then wire it into your home's electrical system. Once the AEG is up and running, you won't even notice . . . ."

She cut him off with a raised hand. "No, no. I mean, how does it work? Where does the power come from? Does it run on some kind of petroleum byproduct? Liquid coal? A biofuel?" She paused and lowered her voice. "It's not nuclear, is it?"

"No, ma'am, it's none of those things," Kai answered, but went no further.

Gillian fished for more. "All right, so how does it actually work? Where's the power come from?"

He looked away, peering out the window toward his van. "I really don't know, ma'am. Anything I'd say to try and explain it would be wrong and I wouldn't want to leave you with incorrect information."

"Give it your best shot, then."

"Can I be honest with you, ma'am?" Kai asked, perching on his elbows and leaning over the table. "I was never that good at science, all right? I mean, I'm just a sales guy. I know how to figure out which AEG is right for a particular home and basically how the hookup works. Anything else? That's proprietary, a trade secret. They don't share those with us."

Gillian sat back in her chair and thought for a moment. "It kind of sounds like magic."

That prompted a nervous laugh. "Yes, ma'am, it does a little bit, doesn't it? The tech guys know more about it than I do, as you would expect. I'm sure they're on the ball." There was an awkward silence. Kai seized the opportunity with abandon. "Would you like me to bring a unit inside and show it to you? They're not much to look at, honestly, but it might clear up any confusion you're having. I just have to run out to the van."

Gillian was starting to think that would be a good idea. "Yeah, why don't you do that," she said. Kai nodded and walked out the front door, closing it behind him.

Gillian went back to the couch and grabbed the tablet she had been using when she nodded off. "Phone," she said. Her first instinct was to call Bianca, but she quickly reconsidered. She would tell Gillian to stop being silly, to send away the nice young con man, and they would talk about this when she got home. She was too skeptical to be open-minded about something like this. If it really worked, it would make their lives so much better. "Cancel."

Out the front window she could see Kai fishing around in the back of the van. "Internet search," she said and turned the tablet sideways to utilize the wide screen. "Search terms: Infinity . . . power . . . AEGs." After a few seconds a screen appeared with a list of search results. She touched the link for Infinity's corporate page. Like Kai's van it had a simple black background with the infinity symbol prominently featured. She found a link called "About AEGs" and clicked it. It opened a page full of the same kind of information that Kai had provided, but nothing about how they worked. She scrolled back and then clicked on the link for "Contact Us." Instead of a physical address or phone number, all that was provided was a form to fill out that would send an email to the company.

She backed up and looked at the other search results. The next link was for one of those review sites where people groaned and complained about every product under the sun. She clicked on it and was presented with a few dozen reviews for Infinity Energy Services. She scrolled quickly through them. All were positive, most five stars out of five. Even the few four-star reviews were gripes about a technician showing up a few minutes late. There were no real complaints, no one-star screeds about how Infinity stole their money or how AEGs were a scam.

As she scrolled back to the top of the site, she saw Kai heading back to the front door. "Shit," she muttered to herself. "Power off." The tablet's screen went blank.

She opened the door and Kai walked through, straight back to the kitchen. On the table he placed a rectangular box, about two feet high and one-and-one-half feet on all sides. It was black with the company logo on the front, in line with the now-familiar corporate theme. Just below the logo was an on/off switch. Aside from that, the box didn't look like much of anything.

"This is our mid-range model, ma'am, the AEG 750," Kai said with pride. "Based on the size of your house I think this model would completely take care of your energy needs."

Gillian could picture it in the garage, maybe buried under a pile of rags, humming away in the dark. "What do the numbers mean?"

Kai chuckled. "Nothing technical, ma'am. Those are the prices for the down payment."

"Down payment?"

"Yes, ma'am. It's more of a lease arrangement than a straightforward purchase. There would be an initial down payment for the AEG 750, followed by a low monthly maintenance fee, around a hundred dollars."

"A hundred bucks?" Gillian asked without thinking, a reflex triggered by the low price.

"Yes, ma'am," Kai said, smiling. "I take it from your response that you pay significantly more per month for energy now?"

Gillian nodded, still a bit dumbfounded. They were still paying off the installation costs of the solar panels, not to mention the monthly fees to Vandalia. Their total energy bill was easily six times Infinity's fee every month. Even figuring in the initial cost of installation, it was a hell of a deal. "The monthly fee is for maintenance?"

"Yes, ma'am."

"What's involved with that? Can't we do it ourselves?"

"No, ma'am, I'm afraid not. Part of the contract, you see, is that only licensed and authorized Infinity techs can open up the case and see what's inside. Proprietary technology, as I said before."

Gillian nodded. "I bet we have to sign up for a certain period of time, right? What is it? A year? Thirty months?"

"No, ma'am," Kai answered, shaking his head. "You may terminate the contract at any time."

Kai was giving her all the right answers. "Can I get a demonstration?"

"No, ma'am, I'm sorry. The system only works after it's been integrated with your electrical system. I don't have the knowledge or authority to do an installation just for a demonstration." He shrugged his shoulders as if to emphasize his helplessness.

"Honestly, Kai, what you're saying is very tempting." It would make such a huge difference in their budget Bianca wouldn't mind that Gillian gave in to a door-to-door salesman. "But I can't help feeling that there's something you're not telling me. It just sounds too good to be true. I mean, I'm pretty on the ball when it comes to cutting edge stuff, but I've never heard of Infinity before today, or an AEG."

"Infinity started up 11 years ago as a small start-up in Oregon," Kai said, obviously launching into a preprogrammed spiel. "The company spent five years developing the AEG technology, first on a smaller scale and then slowly moving into residential applications. We've been installing them all over the country for the last four years."

"With no advertising? No news reports?" Gillian asked.

"Our founder and CEO believes in growing slowly and building strong relationships with customers one at a time. It doesn't work to make bold promises that aren't kept. Much better to convince people, face-to-face, of the benefits of AEGs. Once a customer sees and feels how well an AEG works, they're a customer for life. Tell you what, though. I can see you're a little concerned about the whole thing, and I don't blame you."

"You're just asking me to take a lot on faith," she said. "I mean, how do I know that if I write you a check today, you won't disappear and I'll never see you again?"

Kai raised a hand. "No payment due until the unit is installed, ma'am."

"All right," she said, spinning out the next scenario, "then how do I know that once the unit is installed we won't be out the down payment and left with a useless black box?"

Kai looked at her for a moment, then put down the clipboard. "All right, ma'am, I'm not supposed to do this and I never have, but you sound like you're very interested in an AEG and I wouldn't want to leave without doing all I can to make this happen. I suppose I could provide a small demonstration." He picked up the box and turned it around. On the back was a three-prong outlet, just like one on any wall in the house. "Do you have something you could plug in there?"

"Sure," Gillian said. She grabbed a spare charging cord for her tablet and handed it to him.

Kai took the cord and plugged one end into the AEG. "Really, ma'am, I'm not supposed to do this, so . . ." He let his sentence drift off as he flipped the power switch.

Gillian didn't hear anything, aside from the click of the switch. "Is that it?"

Kai nodded toward the tablet. Gillian picked it up and plugged the power cord into it. The screen came briefly to life, announced that it was charging, then went black again. It was working.

"Convinced, ma'am?"

Try as she might, Gillian could no longer resist the inevitable. "Yeah, I guess so." She could hear Bianca chiding her for giving in, but it was such a good deal. It would cut their costs so much and relieve so much tension. Gillian wanted to find a catch, she just couldn't.

"Great. I'll be right back," Kai said and walked briskly back to the van. When he returned, he was scrolling and tapping furiously on a white tablet that was about twice the size as Gillian's.

They sat back down at the kitchen table. Kai scrolled through the document on the tablet, pointing out the relevant information about Gillian's location, prices, and other mundane matters. Then he handed it to her. "The rest of this is mostly legalese. Boilerplate type stuff, an end user license agreement, like for a piece of software. Scan over it and sign at the bottom," he said, handing her a stylus.

Gillian scrolled through the paragraphs of text, set forth in large shapeless blocks, with care. In college she signed a credit card contract without reading the fine print and her credit report still had problems because of it. She had learned her lesson the hard way. To her relief, however, it looked like Kai was right. The EULA talked about various procedural items that likely would never come up and certainly weren't deal breakers. Nonetheless, her sluggishness seemed to get to Kai a little bit.

"If you have any questions, ma'am, just ask," he said after a few minutes.

"No, no," Gillian answered without looking up. "I'm fine."

A few more minutes passed. "Like I said, it's mostly things we've already gone over," Kai said.

"I can see that," Gillian answered. "Give me time. I'm a slow tablet."

"Really, ma'am," Kai spoke up again after a few minutes, "I hate to be this way, but I do have other appointments today. I'm already running behind thanks to the demo. If there is something you're having a problem with . . ."

Gillian cut him off. "How about this?" she asked, pointing to a paragraph near the bottom of the page. It was the next to last before the lines for her signature and the date, perfectly positioned to be skipped over in frustration of all that came before but far enough away from the end to not be in the field of vision when signing.

"What's that, ma'am?"

"It's this paragraph here that ends," Gillian started reading from the form, "'any party to this contract, and any person present in the home where the Unit is installed, waives all rights to seek legal recourse in the case of Unit malfunction.' What's that about?"

If Kai was put on the defensive by this, he didn't show it. "That's a standard legal disclaimer and waiver. Products of all kinds have them. Nothing special."

"Nothing special? My tablet might overheat or my dishwasher might flood the kitchen. What happens if this mystery box malfunctions? What is so bad that we sign away all our rights?"

"With all due respect, ma'am, none of those things are as valuable as your AEG," Kai responded with trained precision.

"That's not the point," she said. "What happens if this thing breaks down? Is it going to zap the whole neighborhood out of existence?" She chuckled at her absurd scenario.

Kai was not laughing. He stood stock still and swallowed, hard.

"I was joking," Gillian said. "For God's sake, was I right?"

Kai's eyes flitted around the room, as if he was trying his best to look at anything other than her. "In the decade or so since AEGs first went on the market, there has never been a failure. Not one. Between our regular maintenance and upgrades to the units as needed, there really isn't anything to worry about."

"You must have an odd definition of 'worry.' I'm sorry, but I can't be a part of this."

"Why not?" Kai asked, oddly cheerful. "We've all been a part of this for years. In the pursuit of comfort or convenience, of cheap power, mankind has done all sorts of risky things. Just watch the news. Coal mines cave in. Nuclear reactors melt down. Wrecked rigs and tankers spew oil out into the ocean. This is no different. Risk versus reward."

"It's quite different," Gillian said.

He didn't let her keep going. "Because this time it's *your* family at risk? Why are you willing to risk the lives of others for your comfort? Why not take the risk yourself?"

Gillian stood up. "Don't try and turn this back on me, you little shit. I'm not the one selling products that could kill people."

"But haven't killed anybody," Kai shot back, standing and snatching his tablet off the table.

"I don't think most people read those things before they sign them," Gillian said, pointing towards the contract.

"That's not my problem," he said with a shrug. "If someone is willing to sign their name to something they haven't read, it's really on their head."

"If that makes you feel better doing your job . . ."

"It's not about me, ma'am," he said. "It's about human nature. We've always been willing to make trade-offs when it comes to comfort. Who's to say that it's not better to live with a slight, infinitesimally small risk of death in return for years and years of cheap abundant power?"

"I am," she said, walked over to the door, and opened it. "Good day."

Kai walked through the door and nodded politely. "Ma'am."

Gillian watched him from the doorway until he got into his van and drove away. He did not stop at another house in the neighborhood. She wondered if that was part of the strategy, so that she would not run right over to her neighbors and interfere with the pitch or make them read the fine print.

The whole encounter left Gillian with a splitting headache. She went back to the couch and lay down, closing her eyes. She thought about a comfortable, cool house and no more fights about money. Then she thought about Bianca and the kids suddenly vanishing into thin air. Gillian shook her head and tried to clear her mind while her temples throbbed. It would be easier if it wasn't so hot.

# Elephant Talk

Anne Davies sat at her desk, fingers poised over the computer keyboard – suspended, hovering in midair. Anne stared at the screen, but her fingers would not move. Writer's block. Again. Most people think it only happens to writers, but lawyers get the acute case now and then, too. Especially when the brief you're trying to write requires some creative verbal and logical gymnastics. Doubly so when your "clients" consist of the furry, the feathered, and the four-legged. Frustrated, Anne dipped her head and gently pounded it on the desk, fingers still at the ready. Just as she thought an idea was about to be jarred loose by the pounding, there was a tentative knock on the door.

"No," thought Anne, "not now. I'm in no mood for his nonsense." The knock came again.

"Yes, what do you want, now, Jim?" Anne said, with more than a hint of frustration.

The door creaked slowly open and Anne's secretary/paralegal/partner in crime cautiously poked his head through. "Uh, Anne, there's . . . um, well . . ."

"What is it?!" Jim regularly tested her patience by merely doing his job.

Jim was obviously nervous, more so than usual, due to Anne snapping at him. Jim was the gung-ho half of Anne's animal law firm, a former PETA activist who decided that he could do more good in a courtroom (and with a steady paycheck) than with a bullhorn and a tub of fake blood. Sometimes, however, Jim's old activist streak led him to bring Anne clients who were more interested in publicity stunts or political causes than solid legal cases. Today was not the right day to bring one of those into the office.

"Well, it's just that . . .," he said, before stopping himself. "You really have to come see for yourself. There's something, uh, someone, out in the parking lot who wants to meet with you."

"Then show him or her in, Jim. Sit 'em in the conference room, give 'em a cup of coffee, and tell 'em I'll be there shortly."

"That won't work, Anne."

"Why the hell not?"

"He won't fit in the conference room."

Anne didn't even ask why. She just pushed her chair back from her desk and walked briskly past Jim to the waiting room window. From there she could see whatever stunt Jim was trying to pull and put him in his place quickly and efficiently. As she walked to the window, she noticed how particularly clear and blue the sky was on this spring day and wanted desperately to be anywhere but in the office. Then she looked down in the parking lot and saw the elephant.

"Jim, I swear to God, this is not funny and I am in no friggin' mood for this. There's a goddamn elephant in the parking lot! Do you have any idea how pissed Dr. Ryan's gonna' be when she gets back from lunch?"

Jim stood his ground. "Anne, believe me, this is not a stunt. It's not of my doing. The elephant found me."

"He found you."

"Yeah."

"And you know this because . . .," Anne trailed off, wanting to see just exactly how insane Jim had become.

"He told me."

Anne looked at Jim with a dumbfounded look on her face. She didn't quite know whether to laugh or cry.

Jim picked up on Anne's skepticism. "Look, I have not gone crazy. He was there when I got back from lunch. He told me that he read a column I wrote in the local paper and noted where I worked. He wants a lawyer."

"Why, pray tell, does this elephant need a lawyer? Has he been charged with a crime? If so, he's the public defender office's problem, not ours."

"He wants to sue the Republican Party," Jim said with a straight face.

Anne could contain herself no longer, letting out a deep, long laugh. She doubled over at the waist, returning to vertical while whipping away tears from her eyes. "He wants to sue the GOP? For what?"

"Libel. Slander. Defamation of character. Says he's tired of elephants being associated with a right-wing political party. Says at least the jackasses can't complain about the Democrats using them, since all politicians are jackasses, anyway."

"You know, that's completely silly," Anne said, launching into lawyer mode. "For one thing, the GOP didn't come up with the elephant symbol, Thomas Nast did. He's long dead and dead men pay no damages. For another, I'm assuming that our mammoth friend out there wasn't the model for Nast's cartoons in the first place. There's no such thing as defamation of species. Not yet, anyway." Anne paused for a second before bringing up the practical problem. "All of that aside, how would we finance that kind of a lawsuit? Jumbo down there obviously has gone AWOL from wherever home was, and I'm fairly certain he doesn't have a slush fund to fuel a lawsuit."

"All that's true," Jim admitted. "But come talk to him anyway. What have you got to lose by talking?"

"All right," Anne sighed, resigning herself to staying late tonight to finish that brief. If that's what it would take to make this go away, so be it. "But I swear on my mother's grave, Jim, if this is some kind of joke of which I am the punch line, I will kick you so hard you won't be making any baby elephants, understand?"

Jim nodded in agreement and started towards the door. Anne looked out the window one last time, just in time to see the beast stinky drop some smelly, stenchful, odoriferous elephant dung right where Dr. Ryan's Audi should be parked.

"Well, isn't that lovely," Anne said as she walked through the door.

# Memory of Water

I'm on the bridge, on the walkway that runs beside the road. Tourists walk along here every day. They pause here and there, taking pictures of the bay, the hills, even the bridge itself. Today it's not crowded and nobody notices when I climb out over the railing. Or nobody cares. It hardly matters.

~~~~~

One night I started having this dream. That's not unusual, in its own right, but this one was particularly vivid. Vivid but unclear, if that makes any sense. What I saw was unmistakable, but I couldn't shake the thought that there was something I was missing. There was definitely a little boy involved. A toddler, maybe a little older. He was in trouble. I couldn't say for certain what kind of trouble, or why he was in it, but the sense that he was in danger was powerful. It lingered with me after I woke up that morning.

I told Sofia about the dream. It's the kind of thing we always talked about over breakfast. She always listened carefully when I talked about dreams, but that morning she seemed more interested than usual.

~~~~~

A few days later I woke up screaming. Sofia and I had fallen asleep on the couch, as we often do. I had been roused out of it so suddenly and so violently that I awoke with a jerk, nearly throwing Sofia to the floor.

It was the dream, again, the one with the little boy. But this time more of the details were clear to me. I could tell there was water, everywhere, but it wasn't like rain. More like standing water. Only it wasn't natural, like a lake or the ocean. Maybe it was a swimming pool? It seemed like a pool, full of deep, still, impossibly blue water. The boy was submerged in it, trapped, unable to move.

After I told Sofia about it, she got up and went back to the kitchen. I thought I heard her crying, but when I asked if everything was all right, she said it was. I wasn't going to argue with her.

~~~~~

After work the next day, Sofia presented me with a list of chores that absolutely had to be finished that evening. The yard needed to be mowed. The pool had to be cleaned. The tree on the corner of the house needed to be cut back. Normally I would have tried to put off those sorts of chores until the weekend, but Sofia insisted. She was so adamant that I went along with her plans. By dinnertime, I was completely worn out.

Then, at the end of all that, Sofia jumped me. I was getting ready for bed, as usual, and there she was in this slinky blue nightie I'd gotten her for something or other years ago. I can't remember the last time she wore it.

We made love like we hadn't in ages. We spent hours lost exploring each other's bodies. I forgot about needing to get to sleep for work in the morning. I forgot about the impending visit from my sister. Everything about the world disappeared except the two of us and our entwined flesh. I think we were too tired to go any further. Sofia fell asleep in my arms. I was more worn out than I'd been for weeks.

~~~~~

I don't remember waking up early that morning. I don't remember walking to the sliding door, opening it, and walking out onto the patio. Yet, somehow, I wound up sitting on the side of our swimming pool. I said it was pointless to buy a house with a pool. The maintenance would be a pain; the insurance would be expensive. I don't even like to swim. But Sofia loved it and it was nice for entertaining. I was sitting there, balled up, knees under my chin, staring into the water.

I realized that was what it looked like, the water in my dream. It was the same color blue. That clear, crystal blue that you only find in swimming pools, at least in this country. It was the water in the dream. The water that engulfed the boy. The water that drew him under, silently screaming as it filled his lungs, howling impotently for someone to help. But I couldn't. In the dream all I could do was watch.

Sofia came outside, worried about me, said she didn't know where I was. I told her she shouldn't be so concerned. There were plenty of mornings that I got up before she did. I told her about the dream, the new details I remembered. About the water.

By then the sun was coming up. It was time to go to work.

~~~~~

That afternoon I found the box.

I had gone to work, like any other day, but quickly developed a splitting headache. The meeting Mike and I were supposed to have with new clients in the afternoon got cancelled, so I came home. My head felt like it was going to split open. I took some pills and lay down on the couch. The pain subsided, but only by a little. I couldn't relax or doze. My mind was restless.

So I wandered around the house. I wound up in the basement. I couldn't say why. All that was down there were things put away in storage. In the corner was a small drafting table and a stool we had in our first apartment. I can't remember why we didn't give it to Goodwill years ago.

I started looking at all the things piled up in the basement, all the boxes. I didn't look in them; there was no need. Somehow, I knew I wasn't interested in most of them. They didn't hold anything I didn't already know. They were stacked neatly, but accessibly. Some didn't have lids, so I could peek inside if I wanted.

In the corner of the basement, under a stack of books and magazines, there was another box. I cleared away the clutter at the top and looked at it for a minute. It was sealed shut with packing tape, layers of it like it had been opened and sealed repeatedly. Nothing on the outside indicated what might be inside it. I lifted it off the floor and moved it over to the drafting table. It wasn't very heavy. I carried it back upstairs and set it on the couch.

I went to the garage and found the box cutter I kept in my tool box. With it, I was easily able to slice through the layers of packing tape that sealed the box. That barrier removed, I lifted off the top and looked inside.

It was filled with a jumbled collection of papers. Pictures, documents, letters, notes. They were all about a boy. His name was Terry. When he was four years old, he had drowned. According to a police report in the box, he'd fallen into a backyard swimming pool. He'd been left alone and just wandered into the water. His father tried to save him, but by the time he got there, it was too late.

There was no doubt in my mind. It was the boy. The boy from my dreams was in the box.

Terry was my son. Here, in the box, was his birth certificate. It had my name on it. It had Sofia's name on it. And it had Terry's name on it. The boy in my dreams was my son.

~~~~~

Sofia came home early. I was sitting on the couch with the box beside me when she got here. It was mostly empty, its contents strewn about the floor in front of me. I held a picture of Terry, taken a few days before he died. Sofia looked mortified.

She confirmed what I had learned from the box. We had a son. When he was four years old, he drowned out in the backyard pool. We were getting ready for a party, and I had stepped inside to do something, leaving Terry out by the pool by himself. I had meant to go right back out but got sidetracked and lingered too long. By the time I returned he was in the pool, floating lifelessly in the water. I tried to save him, but by then it was too late.

Sofia told me I didn't remember any of this because she had a mnemonic block put in my brain shortly after it happened. She said I was so upset about what happened that I was suicidal. I blamed myself. I had to be committed, which allowed her to make the decision to have the block put in. She said she did it because she couldn't stand to lose me, too, just after she had lost her son.

I don't remember any of that, but I suppose I wouldn't. I had to trust Sofia. But maybe I shouldn't? By her own admission, she had been hiding this from me for nearly five years. How could I trust someone who had admitted to messing with my mind? And why, if she was so concerned about me, did she leave the box in the basement? I asked her, but she just got angry and said something about she had a right to remember. Apparently I didn't.

Sofia told me that the people at the institute explained how sometimes the blocks break down and the memories come back as dreams. All that had happened a few nights before – the chores, the sex – was an attempt to get me into a sleep so deep the dreams would stop. She said I could go back to the institute and have a new block installed and hope it wouldn't break down later. Or I could just let it fade away and try to live with these memories. She wanted me to have the new block installed, but of course she would say that. It would justify her decision the first time.

I told Sophia I needed some time to figure out what to do. She wanted to talk about it over dinner. She wanted to talk about it before we went to bed. I told her just to leave me alone to figure it out for myself. I went to sleep on the couch, alone.

~~~~~

There were no dreams that night. None that I remembered, at any rate. I don't know if it was because I knew everything now or if the dreams just skipped a night. It didn't really matter. In the small hours of the morning, as I tossed and turned on the couch, I realized what I had to do. Sofia wasn't going to like it.

I told her I wasn't going to have a new block put in. Whatever these memories did to me, I don't want to forget them now. She didn't just take away the memory of Terry's death, but his entire life. Nearly four years of my existence turned into a black hole. All the good was gone along with the bad. I decided I couldn't go on living with that, whatever that meant. That decision upset Sophia.

She was even more upset when I told her that I was leaving. That day. There was simply no way I could continue living with her. Not now. Maybe, sometime in the future, I could come back. Or maybe I wouldn't. I couldn't trust someone who would meddle with my memories, even with the best of intentions. I packed a pair of bags and walked out to the car. Sophia was sitting at the kitchen table, crying.

~~~~~

The days after I left the house were a blur.

I didn't have anywhere to go, at first. I'm sure I could have crashed with Mike for a while, but I didn't want to burden him. I needed to be alone, anyway, to work through things. I found a room at a local hotel, not too expensive but not a dump, either. It was home until I figured out what to do.

Sofia kept calling my cell phone. I turned it off, just to avoid the constant ringing. I checked it every couple of hours to make sure nobody else was trying to get hold of me. The phone in the hotel room rang one morning, but I let it go through to voice mail. It was Sofia, as I expected. Mike probably told her where I was. I didn't blame him, but it complicated things. I called down to the front desk and told them not to give out my room number to anyone.

The good news was that the dreams stopped. There were no more restless nights punctuated by terror. The bad news was that the memories of Terry and what happened to him traveled with me throughout the day. I went to work, but didn't get anything done. Mike was a good friend. He picked up the slack and kept everything running. The firm would do well if he was in charge.

My sister, Amy, was in the hotel lobby when I came home from work one afternoon. She was worried about me, she said, and about Sofia, too. I wondered, if push came to shove, which of us she cared about more. Amy dragged me to dinner, mostly to try and convince me to forgive Sofia for whatever she had done. They were obviously on the same side in this. I tried to make Amy understand how I felt, but I just wound up frustrated and tired. So many days, that was how I felt.

~~~~~

I'm on the bridge. There is a surprising amount of room on the outside of the railing, which is not high enough to keep people from doing what I've just done. My feet find a firm place on the sun-bleached steel. I will not slip.

There is a slight breeze. It's cool on my face, on the bare skin of my arms. The sun has slipped behind the full white clouds that dot the sky. It is a beautiful day. I close my eyes and feel the wind against my cheeks. There are voices nearby. I can hear them, but can't make out what they're saying. It doesn't matter.

I open my eyes and look down. Hundreds of feet below, the water of the bay swirls around the bridge supports, dirty green with spurts of white foam. My thoughts drift to the current, the undertow, for just a moment. It will hardly matter what the undertow might be like, I realize, once I hit the water. I chuckle, under my breath, and close my eyes once more.

I'm sorry, Terry. I'm so, so sorry.

# The Last Ereph

The cobblestones that paved these byzantine back alleys were not as clean as they appeared. Kol discovered this when his left foot, rather than pivoting him crisply to the right towards the open alleyway, instead slid out from under him. He did not fall. He managed to catch himself with his right hand. It stung, but was not broken.

More pressing, the slip caused him to lose momentum and provided the chance for one of his pursuers to loose an arrow towards him. It missed, but not by much, flying close enough that Kol could hear it zip past his left ear. Too close.

Kol took just enough time to glance over his shoulder and count--only two of them now. Still enough to catch him. Still enough to kill him. He regained his footing and sprinted down the alley.

Why did he always let people talk him into these things? On the surface they were wrong, but his friends always managed to convince him. "It's for the best," they said. "It must be done," they said. "It is the right thing to do," they said. If that is all true, then why did the duty to act always fall on him? Why would none of his friends ever risk their own skin? No one could ever explain that, on the few occasions Kol was bold enough to ask.

And this time, doing the "right thing" had the Corps of Constables chasing him like hounds after a hare. Whoever this gem belonged to, they were close enough to the His Eminence to have all his power deployed to retrieve it.

He could not outrun them. Kol knew, as a petty thief, that most of his marks, if they pursued him all, had no stomach for a prolonged chase. They would give up in five minutes at the most. It had already been fifteen minutes since Kol snatched the gem and the hue and cry went up. Two of his immediate pursuers had fallen away, but others would no doubt appear from who knows where.

What he needed was to disappear into one of the locked doors of the shops that lined the alley. All were closed and empty, thanks to the feast day. And Kol had never been a lock picker, only a thief. Picking locks seemed so much worse to him than merely taking something that was already available. He would be angry if someone picked the lock of his small room by the wharf. If someone took something because he left the window open, however, he could hardly blame them.

He kept running. The alley jogged left then right, so Kol followed, deftly clipping the apexes of the corners. The next turn lay about two hundred feet in front of him, a sharp right around which the alley disappeared from sight.

Directly in front of him, sunken into the wall at the end of the alley, was a door. This would be Kol's best chance. If it did not work, at least the attempt should not slow him down too much. The jog, about 150 feet behind him now, should provide him some cover if the door did give way. If it did work, he would disappear as if into thin air, for all his pursuers knew.

Kol took a deep breath as he reached the end of the alley and flung himself into the door. As if by a miracle, it gave way. The surprise of success caused Kol to fall face first onto the dark, cool, stone floor inside. He had just enough time to recognize his good fortune before leaping towards the door, back first, to slam it shut.

He sunk to the ground, back against the closed door and the street outside. He held his breath, even though his heart was pounding, listening. There were footsteps. They did not stop. Instead, Kol heard them come and go, taking the turn and continuing down the alley. He was safe.

Kol exhaled and closed his eyes. Only for a moment, he told himself. Just to catch his breath.

~~~~~

When he awoke, Kol's shoulder throbbed. It quickly reminded him of how he had gotten into this place. Which was where, exactly? He needed someplace he could stay, if only until nightfall. Once the sun went down, the Corps would have a harder time tracking him. Perhaps they would have given up by then. He could dump the gem with Ayas and then . . . . Before he could finish his thought, panic gripped him. The gem--was it still here? He fingered the pocket sewn into the underside of his vest and confirmed that the large oblong stone was still there. Kol sighed slightly and looked around.

He sat in a narrow entryway, no wider than the door he had burst through. It was dim, but not completely dark. At first Kol attributed the dull amber light in the entryway to sunlight streaming through windows in the adjacent room. But the light was not consistent, nor did it all appear to be coming from the same direction. Rather, it flickered and danced like candlelight. On a feast day? Who would possibly be in their shop on a feast day? And surely no one would leave candles lit in the shop while it was closed. At any rate, Kol suspected that he was not alone.

He stood up and braced himself against the wall along the left side of the entryway. It was barely wide enough to accommodate one man. Two men passing each other would be out of the question. What kind of shop would have such a narrow entryway? He stepped forward a few paces into the room just ahead of him and strained his eyes against the dimness.

The room was large and ornate, with a high vaulted ceiling. A grimy skylight at the peak of the roof allowed only a little sunlight to enter the room. In the middle of the room was a small stone fountain, although Kol could not hear any water running. Around the outside of the room, built into the walls, was a row of low wooden benches. At the far corner of the room was a raised platform of some kind. Beside it, holding a flickering lantern, was a short old woman. In the candlelight Kol had almost overlooked her. Now he could only make out her long white hair, which appeared to blend seamlessly into the robes she was wearing.

"Greetings, young friend," she said in a voice that rang through the room like a bell. She raised the lantern to her face. She was not smiling, but still appeared to be of a pleasant disposition.

"Hello," Kol said in return, as usual at a loss for words. There was an awkward pause. "I can leave, if you want."

"There is no need for that, young friend," the woman said as she began shuffling towards him. Kol thought he heard her cough.

"Do you not care why I bust through the door a few minutes back?" Kol asked, somewhat bewildered.

"A few minutes?" the woman said and chuckled. "A few hours, more like it." The chuckle turned into a cough.

"I've been here that long?"

"Yes, young friend. You must have been exhausted from whatever brought you here."

"And you don't care about the door?" Kol asked.

"No permanent damage was done," the woman said as she continued towards him. As the old woman moved, the light of her lantern moved with her. Kol could see a bit of still water in the fountain. "Besides," the woman said, "I am in no condition to turn away anyone." A cough clipped the end of her sentence.

"Are you ill?" Kol asked.

"Yes, young friend," she said, her words punctuated by another cough. "Quite so." As she moved closer to him Kol could finally see her face in the full lantern light and knew it to be so. She was hunched over and her gait made her appear brittle, as if her body might simply give way under the strain of living. Her long hair shone almost like silver in the lantern light. Sunken, dark brown eyes dominated her face, which was lined and pitted with the scars of a life long lived. In spite of all that, there was a certain liveliness in the way she carried herself.

"Then why are you here, alone, in this dark place on a feast day?" Kol asked. "Do you have no one to look after you?"

"All I have is this place," she said, waving her free hand around the room. "I take care of it and it takes care of me. As best we can, at any rate." She coughed again.

"This place," Kol had realized was a cult house. Like the dozens of others in the city, it had the purification fountain at its center, a lectern from which lectures were given in one corner, and benches around the outside for the acolytes. In layout it was the same as the cult house of Camiol, in which he was raised and still occasionally made offerings. They never led to anything, he noticed, but old habits die hard. Kol did not recognize the iconography of the carvings in the room. "And what is this place?" he finally asked.

The old woman was standing just in front of him now. "This, young friend, is the Great House of the Cult of Leib."

Kol smiled, politely. "Is it really?" he said. The old woman was obviously not only sick, but senile, as well. Each cult had one Great House, usually in the city in which the cult began. Some might be moved to a city where the cult was very popular, but this Cult of Leib was anything but popular. Kol had never heard of it before. And he knew that Seay had nothing in its history so grand as the founding of a cult. While not an isolated trading post, Seay was near the very edge of the empire, far away from the bustling hub of Soltoh. It was not the kind of place where one would find a Great House.

The old woman looked at him. Some aggravation, or perhaps merely amusement, crept across her face. "Yes, young friend. Really. Why do you look at me with such doubt in your eyes?"

Kol walked over to the fountain, the old woman and her lamp light in tow. He could see now that it was one-third full with tepid water. "Well, for one thing, I've never heard of this Cult of Leib before. And I've lived in Seay since I was born. I was never told that the city gave birth to a cult. And, well," he gestured to the empty hall, "look at this place. Take no offense, but this does not look like any kind of Great House."

The old woman chuckled at him and coughed, then shuffled across the room and took a seat on the bench. "What if I told you, young friend, that none of what you say is inaccurate, yet you are still wrong to doubt me?"

Kol walked over and sat beside her. "I'd say I still don't believe you, but I could be convinced. My name is

Kol, by the way." The instant he said it he knew it was a mistake. He was still running from the Corps, a stolen gem of unknown value pressed against his chest. Now he had told this strange woman his real name. He hoped it would not be the end of him.

"Peace be upon you, Kol. I am Reynar, last ereph of the Cult of Leib."

"Last?" he asked.

"Yes," Reynar said. "That is perhaps why you have never heard of us. And never would have, had you not burst through the door this day."

"I suppose so," Kol said. "What happened to your flock, then? Where are your acolytes? Were your people persecuted?" It was well known that the cults of the emperor and his closet advisors or those who won famous military victories, enjoyed consummate surges in popularity. What was less obvious, or perhaps just more easily ignored, was that with changes in emperors or costly military defeats came a change in the cults of favor. Those then out of favor and identified with political opponents were often harassed and sometimes brutally purged. Many cults died out under such pressure.

"Oh, no," Reynar said. "The Cult of Leib, although ancient and influential in thought, has never held the favor of an emperor. It was never one of the more fashionable cults. The most famous of our members, I suppose, was Orvin."

"The hero of Maehlen?" Kol asked. At Maehlen, Orvin had organized a beaten and ragged legion and led them in a counterattack that turned the tide of the battle.

But that was over seven centuries ago. In this age, Orvin's exploits were more legend than history.

"Yes, although he was only an acolyte at the time."

"He could have been emperor, had he wished it," Kol said.

"I do not know the specifics," Raynar said. "Nor are they important. But I believe that Orvin did not want such power in his hands. He was a reluctant leader, the kind that often acts wisely but does not seek to expand his influence or even maintain what influence he gains."

"Is that what happened to your cult? It never had a great leader?"

"No, not really," Raynar said. "There have been many brilliant leaders in our past, beginning with Leib himself, of course. But they never sought political influence and never found great favor amongst the governing class. At times that seemed like a wise course, insulating us from the swirls and jolts of politics. But it also limited our reach, for which we are now paying dearly."

Kol thought about that for a moment before continuing. "I can understand staying out of politics. I have little use for it myself," he said, making a joke that was poorly received. "But if the cult has dwindled to only have one member, why not recruit new ones? Have you not gone to Speaker's Square and sought new members?" Speaker's Square was a good spot for Kol. Lots of people standing around being interested in anything but their own pockets or parcels.

Raynar looked at him with a wan smile. "That is the problem, you see, young friend. Leib was very explicit about his way."

"I don't understand," Kol said. "What's the point of founding a cult if you're not going to try and bring new members into it? Unless it was some kind of secret society."

"Piffle," Raynar said, with a cough. "Secret societies are a myth, young friend. Think about it – have you ever heard of a secret society?"

"Sure. The Watchers. The Coastliners. Everybody knows about them."

"Precisely," she said, jabbing a trembling finger towards him for emphasis. "Once everyone knows about them, they are hardly a secret, are they? Humans are simply no good at keeping secrets. Groups of humans even less so." She shifted her approach. "You are a thief, aren't you, young friend?"

Kol stiffened for a minute, fighting an urge to run for the door or just deny the accusation. But if the old woman was telling the truth and she was alone here, he would have no problem keeping her silent. If it came to that. "I suppose I am."

"You suppose nothing. Either you are or are not, and I already know you are, so don't bother arguing with me."

It was only then that Kol became aware that he had been grasping the gem in his pocket since they sat down. "I wouldn't dream of it," he said.

"Well said. Now, you must have friends or associates. Other thieves, I imagine, with whom you share your burden."

No point in being coy now. "Actually, I have friends and then there are other . . . thieves that I know, but they are not the same."

"All the better," Raynar said in an excited tone. "What you and your thieving friends discuss is crime, punishable by all sorts of horrible dictates of His Eminence. Discovery of your activities is something to be avoided, yes?"

"Of course."

"But your friends know of your ways, do they not?"

"Most of them," Kol said.

"You see, my point proven. Of all people, Kol, you have a rational reason to keep your thievery a secret, at least from the law abiding, yet you do not. Given your experiences, how would secret societies survive for any length of time?"

Kol did not see any reason to argue the point and decided to move on. "OK, so the Cult of Leib was not a secret society. Then why have I never heard of you before and why are you its last ereph?"

"As I was saying, before our little detour," Raynar said with obvious enjoyment, "Leib was very explicit about his way. He taught us to be generous with our time, energies, and knowledge when confronted by those interested in our ways. But he taught that it was unseemly and . . . well, rude, would be the best word . . . to go out and seek to force our way on others."

Kol snickered, even though he tried to avoid it.

"That was not a joke, young friend," Raynar said, with obvious confusion.

Kol quickly apologized. "I'm sorry. It's just that the idea of a cult being directed not to recruit new members. It's just not how the world works."

"What if it is the way it should work?" Raynar said, scolding him. "Did you ever think of that, young friend? There are more important things in this world than how many followers one can claim."

"Fair enough," Kol said, "but don't you need to have some followers to keep the cult going? What about children? They're taught the cult's ways while growing up, right?"

Raynar shook her head. "You do not understand. Leib taught that true wisdom and understanding can only come about from free choice made after considering all the arguments. To indoctrinate children in our ways would keep many of them from making such a choice."

"So you don't even hold on to the children?"

"We encourage children to learn about many different cults, and to even consider the views of those who have no cult at all. When they are young adults, they go out into the world to experience its many ways and customs. Some come back and join the Cult of Leib and are fully committed to its ways."

"But what of the others?" Kol asked. "If only some returned to this house, then many more must have left."

Raynar let out a long sigh and sat for a minute, silent, as if fully absorbing Kol's blow. "That is correct, young friend. Sadly, many of the other cults teach blind obedience and focus on the accumulation of power or wealth or influence. Leib valued knowledge above all else, along with thoughtful reflection in all affairs. It is, I think, the best way to order one's life. But it is not a very popular view."

Kol could hear the sadness in the old woman's voice. He had known true believers before, those that were so convinced of their own righteousness that they would brag about it to anyone at anytime. These outspoken cultists were loud, boorish, and frequently dangerous. But Raynar seemed to be the opposite of all that. "Are you telling me, Raynar, that you are the last of your kind because you chose not to force your beliefs on anyone, including your own children, and therefore your members slowly chose to join other cults?"

Raynar's silence provided the answer.

"That is so depressing," Kol finally said, his low voice echoing around the nearly empty chamber. "It's just not fair."

Raynar let out a quick snicker that became a longer wracking cough. "Life, as they say, young friend, is not fair. Were it so, I would not be counting out my final days with this consumptive cough."

Kol placed a hand gently on the old woman's shoulder. "I've never liked the cults," he said. "They were always about getting new members. Pestering people to join their house and give them their goods. Cults would split up a family if it meant a new member, especially a young one. They're all about trying to get you to do something you know deep down in the pit of your stomach you shouldn't. Not because it's immoral or a sin, or whatever. Just because . . . well, because it's a lousy way to treat people."

Raynar looked at him sympathetically. "I thought you did not belong to a cult, young friend? You sound as if you bear its scars."

"Thinking about it, about how the other cults behave. They remind me a lot of my friends," Kol said, his voice trailing away as he finished. "They are all the time trying to get me to do things. Dumb things. Or, at least, things that aren't very bright."

"Like stealing whatever it is you're hiding inside your vest?" Raynar asked.

Kol slipped his hand into his pocket and slid the smooth lemon-sized gem from his its hiding place. Its light weight belied its size. He held it out in the palm of his hand so Raynar could see it. "It's really quite beautiful," he said. "The light in here does not do it justice. When the sunlight hits it just so . . ."

The old woman cut him off. "If it is so beautiful why would you take it from someone else?"

"Because my friends told me," Kol said before he stopped himself. "No. That's not right. Because, well,

I'm not really sure. I suppose I let myself be convinced that the woman from around whose neck it hung did not deserve to have it." He shrugged.

"Do you have a family to support? Children? Someone more deserving of such riches?"

"No," Kol said, hanging his head. "I don't have anyone."

"You have your friends," Raynar said. "I can see that they have a lot of influence upon you."

"Too much," Kol said. "Too much. I guess that's why what you say about your cult is so depressing. You did things the right way. You didn't take advantage of others who were in need or confused about their path in life. You let only those genuinely interested in Leib's teaching become members. And this is how you are repaid," he said, waving his empty hand around the nearly empty chamber.

"A life well lived is payment enough, young friend. What do you think the purpose of any cult is? To try and frame the world in a way which allows its members to live the fullest of lives. I have had many wonderful encounters since I became ereph with those who sought to know Leib's teachings. Some came into the cult for a number of years before moving on. Some to other cults. Others simply passed on. I have no regrets about my work, young friend. Do not pity me."

"I won't," Kol said, looking at her. "I don't. But doesn't it make you sad or angry or something to know that all this comes to an end when you're gone?"

"I don't pretend to know the future. It is true, I am not a well woman. But many in my condition live for years. Who is to say I will not? And who is to say that in whatever time I have left someone else will not come seeking the teachings of Leib and become my successor?"

"Successor?"

"Why not?" Raynar asked with a look surprise. "I am the last ereph simply because there is no one else to do the job. That description, like many things in life, is always open to redefinition."

Kol chuckled and tried to keep his mind from going where it was headed. He changed the subject. "Raynar, I've lived in Seay all my life and never heard of the Cult of Leib or that the city hosted a great house. If Leib was not from Seay, how did the great house come to be here?"

Raynar shifted gears swiftly. "No, the cult did not begin here. Leib was living in Milton when he started his cult. He spent many afternoons in the Speaker's Square listening to the erephs debating and recruiting for their cults. Have you ever been to Milton?"

Kol shook his head. He had only ever been about a day's ride from Seay.

"I was born there. Long after Leib, of course," she said with a shallow chuckle. "It is a magnificent city. So full of life and variety. Speaker's Square there is four, no five, times the size of the one here in Seay. And crowded beyond belief, at that." She paused for a moment, as if lost in a memory of that age.

"And?" Kol asked, prodding her to continue.

"I'm sorry," she said, shaking her head. "I went away there for a moment. Where was I?"

"Leib was in Speaker's Square in . . ."

"Yes, yes, yes," Raynar interrupted him, waiving her hands to stop his progress. "Like you, Leib was not enamored of the way the erephs in the square behaved. Cults seemed most concerned primarily with their own continued existence and filling their houses. Each sniped at the other over minor things, but never endeavored to actually engage on the vital issues. 'How can we double our membership?' was more interesting to them than 'Why are we here?' or 'What is the meaning of life?'"

"So he formed his own cult?"

"Not at first. He joined several already established cults, first to confirm his suspicions about them--which were true--and then to see if they could be changed from the inside. It was only when he concluded that fundamental change required a clean slate that he started the Cult of Leib."

"And that was in Milton"

"No. To do that he went to Igton, a port city on the northern coast. It was much smaller than Milton, but it was a major stopping point for ships travelling the Straight of Igbis. That meant there were not as many cults there, and none as viscously competitive as those in Milton, but with many travelers passing through Leib had access to all their tales and reports."

"So why isn't the great house in Igton?"

"Because the reason Leib went there in the first place was the reason it was not the best place to grow such an unconventional cult," Raynar explained. "If Leib had wanted his cult to compete for members the way the others did, he could have quickly become the dominant cult in the city. Having a great house in a city is a great recruiting tool. If you are willing to use it."

"So he moved to a larger city?"

"That's right. First to Cyleenas for a while before he settled in Namie. He died there, surrounded by a few dozen acolytes. The great house stayed in Namie for more than a century. Then it moved, to a few different cities, over the years, as our numbers dwindled. It arrived in Seay about 15 years ago, which is when I joined."

Something had occurred to Kol. "Wasn't all that relocation awfully expensive? I mean, building great houses all over the empire."

"Not really. Thankfully, whether a cult house becomes a great one is due only to whether it is the seat of that particular cult. Nothing more. And you would be surprised how many perfectly serviceable cult houses lay empty around the empire. The Cult of Leib will not be the first, nor the last, cult to disappear." She began to cough again, quietly at first, but it quickly seized her and left her body wracking and filling the chamber with throaty blasts.

As Raynar's fit passed, Kol could no longer avoid the voice in his head that had started up a few minutes before. "Raynar, you said that you would be the last member of the Cult of Leib only so long as someone did not come and take your place before . . . before you die."

The old woman nodded as she caught her breath.

"Let me be the one," Kol said, placing a gentle but firm hand on the old woman's shoulder. "I want to learn the ways of the Cult of Leib."

She removed his hand from her shoulder and shook her head. "No, young friend. I appreciate the offer, but it is born more of pity for me and our cult than a genuine desire to learn Leib's work and continue it. It would not be right."

"I will not lie, Raynar, and say that your situation has not touched me. But that is not why I want to succeed you as the ereph of this great house."

"You must convince me of that," the old woman said. "Why would you give up the life you have known, not just to become a member of a cult, but become its ereph?"

"This life I have known, as you call it. What has it been? A life of petty thievery. Which would be bad enough if I thought it was my calling in life. But I fell into it, because I am good at it, to be honest. My friends were the ones who drove me to it, convincing me always that it was the right thing to do." Kol sighed and looked Raynar in the eyes. "I may have not been in a formal cult all these years, but I've let other people tell me what to do. I don't want that any more. And I don't want a philosophy built around leaving people to their own lives to die out. Is that sufficient?"

"It may be," Raynar said after she thought for a minute. "You still must learn the ways of Leib and decide if they are right for you. But I will teach you. If you are willing to do one thing."

Kol looked at her with a puzzled look on his face. It took a moment before he noticed the old woman's outstretched hand, palm facing up, asking for him to put something in it. Kol held the gem up in front of his eyes. "You think I should give this back, don't you?"

She nodded. "A corollary of the pledge to not cajole people into a life they do not choose is that we cannot simply take from others what we wish. But you cannot simply return it. You would be arrested. Imprisoned. Perhaps worse. If you give it to me, I will be able to return it without any questions being asked."

"Just like that?" Kol asked, surprised at her assertion.

"When you are the ereph of the only great house in a city, it does provide some leverage in such situations," Raynar explained. "If you relinquish the gem, it will be a worthy first step in your learning about the ways of Leib."

Resigned to his choice, Kol gently placed the gem in Raynar's hand. "What now?"

"You will stay here. There are quarters in the back. They will require some work to be made livable, but they will suffice. It is safe, at the least."

"Thank you, Raynar," Kol said, finally, when he found himself at a loss for words.

"Thank you, young friend."

## ABOUT THE AUTHOR

JD Byrne lives in West Virginia with his wife, black cat, and one-eyed dog.  He writes fiction when he's not practicing law.  Contact him on:

The Web: www.jdbyrne.net
Facebook:  www.facebook.com/JDBAuthor
Twitter: @JDBAuthor
Email: jdb@jdbyrne.net